INSUPPRESSIBLE

IN A SMALL TOWN

ALIE GARNETT

For all those raised in a small town, and those who just wish they were.

CHAPTER 1

ALL OF RUSTON ABBOTT'S senses told him this was not the sort of place he should be at. When Thomas had told him they were going to a party, he had expected a small gathering of people his age—not a raging college house party. Sure, Thomas was a year younger than him, but Thomas was still twenty-seven. Even he was too old to be drinking with college kids.

Ruston Abbott and Thomas Harstad had grown up not far from the old two-story house full of young people the party was taking place at. Calling them young people, that should say how old Ruston was right there.

Tonight, they had walked there from his mom and dad's house, that was how close he was to getting home. Thomas had assured him it was going to be a small gathering with friends. If Thomas knew any of these people, he would eat his sock. His friend was a social butterfly, though, so he probably knew them all now.

It was almost 10:00 p.m., and the house was so full of people he could barely move. He should just go back home, leave Thomas behind. The last time he saw the younger man, he had been making out in the corner with a woman Ruston was sure he hadn't known an hour ago.

This was not the sort of place he should be. The music was blaring from the corner of what he assumed was the living room. He had been surprised to see the live band because the house was way too small for that.

Ruston glanced again at his friend in the corner, but he had vanished. Now he was alone in the house full of young people. Young drunk people. How many were underage? How long until the cops were called?

This party could be the end of his career. Ruston knew all it would take was one arrest at a house party full of underage drinkers, and his position at the church would be over—and any other church he wanted to work at. His life would be over, and for what, this?

For the last two years, he had been the preacher at a little church a short two-hour drive from this house. It was a nice little church full of people who looked up to him as a pillar of the community. If he got arrested, that would all be gone.

Why had he stayed this long? Maybe he missed being around rowdy young people just having a good time. Shaking his head, getting his senses back, he knew he was past that time in his life. He was a twenty-eight-year-old preacher now, not a kid.

Turning, he started to make his way to the door to get out of there. As he weaved his way through the large crowd to the door, he realized the band had stopped. The young people had stopped moving to the music, making it easier to get through them. Though not as simple as he would like.

He had almost made it all the way to the door when a new band started. Immediately, he recognized the song from parties he had gone to when he was young, but this was the first time he had heard it as a solo unaccompanied only by a guitar. A woman with a voice like an angel started the first lines of "Life in a Northern Town" with just a lone guitar accompanying her.

Stopping, he turned to see a young woman standing center stage, looking down at the guitar as she played. Her hair was almost white, short, and had been spiked out all over her head. Her makeup was heavy with black rings around her eyes. She was wearing a black tank top and a black leather mini skirt. The army boots were tied loosely on her feet. She looked like a punk rocker, but the song was in contrast to her looks.

His feet were frozen as she continued to sing, slipping into the chorus for the first time; alone and with no support from other band members. As he watched, she looked up from the guitar and scanned the room in front of her. Ruston gasped as her eyes caught his in the crowded room.

Hazel May.

The name ran through his head along with dozens of images of her over the past two years. Every week he saw that face looking back at him from the pews as he preached. Every week she sat next to her grandma and grandpa, Rose and John May. Every week she had her son John on her lap. Every week she had her short blonde hair laying nicely on her head, never standing up like tonight, and she never wore any makeup. She never sang during the songs about God, Jesus, and being saved, but now she poured her heart into this sad song. Her fingers didn't miss a beat; her voice hit every note perfectly. Though he had heard singing every week of his life, he had never heard a voice as serene as hers. He couldn't take his eyes off her as the song came to an end, her hazel eyes on him.

Hazel with the hazel eyes. Hazel with the sad eyes. Hazel, who never smiled.

With the song over, he didn't know what to do. He should leave, but he couldn't walk away from her. On stage, she looked down at the guitar again. When she started the next song, the crowd started to cheer, and Ruston grinned as he saw her smile at their reaction without looking up. Though the song was different with just her playing the guitar, he recognized it as a popular Taylor Swift song on the radio all the time. It was more upbeat than the last one she had played, and some in the crowd sang along as she belted out the song. She didn't catch his eye again as she sang. This time, her eyes kept moving around the room, looking at everyone but him.

As the song came to an end, the band came back on stage, and she handed off the guitar as she jumped down. He lost her in the crowd immediately, as she was not a tall girl. *Woman*, she was a woman. She had a three-year-old son, though he had no idea how old she was.

With the band back on stage, the volume raised as their multiple instruments started their first song. A slow one to get the crowd dancing, he assumed. With a sigh, he turned once again to leave when someone grabbed the back of his shirt and said, "Dance, preacher man."

Turning, he saw the woman who had just held the crowd in her hands, but more importantly, him. Knowing he should leave, he instead turned, following her back into the room to dance with her. There was no way he could say no to her. Pulling her warm, barely clothed body into his arms, he felt her arms go around his neck. He was a little surprised when she rested her head on his chest and that her hair didn't poke into him like the pins it looked like.

Neither said anything as the song played loudly over them. Swaying gently to the music, he didn't even know what to say to the young woman. He was lost for words, but right then, he could barely remember how to put words together.

Why had she wanted to dance with him? Why him, of all people? Had they ever actually talked before?

Pulling away, she lowered her arms from around his neck where her fingers had been tapping to the beat of the music and slid them down to his waist, where she put a hand on either of his hips.

Leaning up so that her mouth was close to his ear, she whispered, "You have no rhythm, preacher man."

He leaned his head down to her ear. "You have enough for both of us."

His heart raced as he watched her laugh. He couldn't hear it over the music, but it made her face light up. At that moment, he knew he had never seen her laugh or smile or sing until tonight. Every week for two years, he had seen no emotion in her.

The song was winding down, and she pulled out of his arms and grabbed his hand. He let her pull him through the crowd. For some reason, he wanted to do whatever she was planning for them. He watched as she looked around a little and then brought him up the stairs in the back of the house. At the top, she led him into the first door she saw.

Once in the room, she turned and pulled him back into the position they had been dancing in when they were in the middle of the crowd. A new song had started, faster than the last, but her movements were the same. He just held her in his arms and danced, letting her set the pace.

With his hands around her waist, they swayed to the music coming through the floor from below. They could barely hear the words, just the bass. He felt her sigh in his arms, and ever so quietly, she started to sing the song the band was playing downstairs. Her fingers drummed in time to the beat on his neck again. It was calming.

When the song ended, a new song came on, but she didn't start singing this one. Instead, without moving her head from his chest, she said huskily, "So, what are you doing here, preacher man? Are you here for the alcohol? The drugs? Sex? All of it?"

"Ruston," he rasped, wanting to hear her say his name.

"Ruston," she repeated after him, mimicking his tone.

"I was here with a friend. He left, I think." Ruston didn't even care anymore; Thomas was old enough to take care of himself.

"Why didn't you leave?" She asked the question he had been asking himself.

"I was going to, but then I heard you singing. I had to stay. You have a beautiful voice, Hazel." They swayed back and forth.

"No, I don't. I just like to sing sometimes." Her words were almost too quiet to hear over the music, but then she started quietly singing the song that the band was playing.

Swaying in a bedroom of a stranger, all he felt was that this was perfect. That all that had happened in his life had led him to this moment, this place. This woman.

As the song ended on a low, sad note, he felt her go still as the band stopped playing. Just holding her in his arms, he had a disconcerting feeling he wanted to kiss her, needed to kiss her. But before he could make a move, she pulled out of his arms as a fast song started up. She started to dance with fast, rhythmic movements that seemed so natural for her and said, "I love this song."

Ruston couldn't tell if he had heard the song before or not. He just stood there trying to decide if he could even dance like she was dancing; he wanted to, but he knew it wasn't as easy as she made it look. After all, she had been right—he had no rhythm.

"Come on, Ruston, dance. Don't make me dance alone." She moved around the room.

"I don't really know how to dance fast," he admitted.

At his words, she stopped in the middle of the room and walked back to where he stood. "Well, first, you look like a preacher man. A little too uptight." She grabbed the button-up shirt he wore and pulled it free from his jeans. Then she unbuttoned the two buttons on top. "There."

"Will that make me dance better?" he teased.

"No, but it will make you not look so out of place." Then she looked into his eyes, and with a sly smile, she reached up and ran her hands through his hair. Cocking her head, she did it again. "Not so uptight now."

With her hands still in his hair, her small body was pressed tight to his. Her every curve pressed into him as those hazel eyes held his while she pulled his head down to hers. Sliding his eyes from hers to her lips, he watched her bite down on that delicate, plump lower lip as she brought his head the rest of the way to her lips.

No gentle kiss for Hazel, he realized immediately as her tongue plunged through his parted lips. Electricity ran through his body as he pulled her tight to him. Had it been so long since he had actually kissed a woman that he instantly needed to feel more of her? Have more of her?

His hands slid up from her waist to her hair—he needed to touch the blonde spikes. To his surprise, they were softer than he had imagined they would be. With his hands on her head, he tilted it so he could have better access to her mouth as their tongues battled.

Feeling her hands leave his hair, she slipped them under his untucked shirt. Over his stomach and chest, they slowly slid, raking her fingernails across his skin as she moved. At his shoulders, she switched directions and sent the nails down his body in the same way they had come.

He knew he needed to stop right now, but the feelings flooding him were overruling his head. Months of celibacy and this woman in his arms won out, and with a groan of defeat, his hands slid from her hair to her shoulders. Then, without thought of what he was doing, he slipped the thin shoulder straps of her tank top and bra strap over her pale shoulders and slid them down her arms. Pulling back from the kiss, his lust-fueled eyes focused on her breasts as they came into view, pink nipples already peaked, temping him to touch. Giving in, he ran a thumb over each one at once and was rewarded by her moan of pleasure.

His mind returned for a moment, and he knew he should stop—had to stop—but when she leaned back, shoving her breasts more into his hands, he decided to wait a moment longer. Enjoy the pale, perky globes for just a bit longer since they were a perfect fit for his hands.

Needing just a simple taste, he leaned down and took one of her nipples into his mouth. Circling it over and over with his tongue, he felt her hands in his hair again. Somehow, she had freed her arms from the sleeves of her tank top and bra and had her hands in his hair, holding his head as if she needed it.

With force, she lifted his head away from her breasts and back to her lips as she plunged her tongue into his again. His hands going to her hips, he ground his ridged cock into her.

Ruston, stop this, his mind said, but his body was overriding his mind as her hand slid under his shirt again. Her nails bit into his skin, and he groaned, mind lost.

Tearing her mouth from his again, she buried her head in his neck and bit down lightly, kissed the spot, and then raised up on her toes and bit his ear lobe. His complete focus was on what her mouth was doing to him, which made him miss what her hands were up to. Until her small hand closed over his cock, hot and firm. Hissing out a breath, he swore as her hand ran from base to tip and back again ever so slowly. Her hand did it again as she plunged her tongue back into his mouth.

All senses were focused on what her hand was doing that he could barely concentrate on the kiss. Her hand motions started to increase, and all he could do was close his eyes, lean his head back and moan. When she stopped abruptly, her thumb caressed the tip, and he hissed a curse. It was then that he felt her tongue replace her thumb as it slid over the tip, and then she blew on it.

He was completely lost as she pushed his pants down until they were at his knees. There was nothing that could make him leave this room right now; his job be damned, he was staying. He was hers as she took him fully into her mouth.

Cursing again, he let her push him over, and he fell flat on his back on the bed behind him. Her mouth never left his erection, never stopping the steady caress of her lips and tongue. On his back, all he focused on was her mouth and watching that spiky hair.

Closing his eyes, he focused on not coming in her mouth, something that he was surprised he could even control anymore. He was out of practice, but she wasn't. As if she could feel he was losing the battle, her mouth gave his tip one last swirl, and she replaced it with her hand again. With slow and steady caresses again, he was getting back some control, so he opened his eyes and pushed up on his elbows, wanting to see Hazel again, needing to see what she was going to do next. Instead, he was met with the scene and sensation of her sliding him into her hot, wet folds. Slowly, he watched as his erection disappeared under her hiked-up leather skirt. The tight, wet feel of being inside her made him swear.

"You say a lot of dirty words when you fuck, preacher man." Her voice was raspy as she started to rock her hips.

"I never have before," he admitted as he watched her throw her head back and increase the tempo. He didn't move, just let her set the pace. Just let her take control. It was all he could do to watch her ride his cock, her eyes pressed closed and her breasts bouncing.

She must have realized that he wasn't moving, just watching her, so she stopped and stared down at him. Then, with both hands, she grabbed his shirt in her fists and pulled herself down so that their mouths were almost touching. She whispered, "Fuck me, Ruston. Fuck me hard."

That was all he needed. Rolling her over so that she was on her back, legs wrapping around him, he started to move—fast. Though his pants were still around his ankles, he wasn't letting it slow him down, and he wasn't taking the time to get them off. Her heels pressed into his lower back, and he realized that at some point she had lost her oversized boots.

When she increased the tempo again, he was okay with her setting the speed. Grabbing her hips as he drove into her, he watched her eyes close and her lips part as her breathing became ragged. She was going to come, and he wanted nothing more than to make it happen. Her hands grasped his hips tight enough to leave marks as she came with a rhythmic chant of, "Yes, yes, yes."

Feeling her walls pulse around him pushed him over the edge, and he came hard. Wave after wave washed through him.

When his body was spent, he collapsed next to her. Breathing heavily, he lay with his eyes closed, but as his heart rate returned to normal, reality started to set in with the beat of the drum from the floor below. He was still at a party, and he had just had sex with Hazel May. Looking back, he wondered how things had that gotten so out of hand. And why was he so happy it had? "What just happened?" She was probably just as shocked as he was.

His words were met with silence, an eerie silence that had a thumping beat. Opening his eyes, he saw the bed was empty. He was alone. Sitting up, he realized the room was also empty.

She was gone.

Her shoes were still there on the floor, but she was gone.

Jumping out of the bed, he pulled up and buttoned his pants. It was only then that he realized he was wearing a condom. He hadn't even realized she had put one on him. That was how out of control he was —he had forgotten about protection.

Grabbing the shoes, he ran out the door. She wasn't there. Downstairs, the house was fuller than it had been before they had gone upstairs. He scanned the crowd, but he didn't see her spiky hair. Pushing past people, he made it to the door but still didn't see her. She was gone.

If it hadn't been for the sensations still floating through his body and her shoes in his hand, he would have thought he had imagined the entire thing. She was gone.

Standing in the yard, he watched for her for a few minutes. Maybe she was still in the house? But he didn't want to go back in there. When she didn't emerge, he tucked the shoes under his arms and started for his parents' house.

It was Friday night. Would she be in her pew on Sunday morning? She was gone now, but he knew that she wouldn't be able to hide from him forever. She was his parishioner.

He had just slept with one of his parishioners at a house party. He should be regretting it but couldn't bring himself to. Not at all.

CHAPTER 2

"WHAT THE HELL HAVE YOU DONE?" Hazel chided herself as she drove out of the city. What was she thinking, having sex with Pastor Ruston? Not just sex, but dirty, fast, hard sex. Damn good sex.

When she decided to go to a party tonight, she had no intention of having sex, just wanted to sing a few songs when the band was on break, then get lost in dancing. For over a year now, she had been following The Swedes Band. They were good, the guitarist was great, and the drummer could actually carry the beat. And when they took breaks, they let her get up and sing—just a few songs, but enough to let her let go and feel something for a moment.

Singing two songs every hour or so was the only way she let go these days; her current life left no room for just being a wild and care-free twenty-three-year-old. She farmed with her grandfather and was a single mother to her John Henry.

So once a month, she drove an hour and a half from Landstad, North Dakota, down the Red River to Grand Forks, North Dakota, and sang her heart out for two songs at a time. She'd leave her son with her grandparents, getting a night of freedom.

But tonight, when she finally had the courage to look up from the guitar to see if anyone was paying attention or if they were just doing their own thing, she had immediately seen him in the crowd. What had drawn her attention to him, she didn't know. But once she saw him, she couldn't take her eyes off him. And he was staring at her also.

For the last two years, he had been the one in the spotlight with her in the crowd just watching him work. Well, it wasn't exactly the same. She sat in a pew with her son on her lap as he talked of God and salvation from the pulpit. He would say the words, but she wasn't listening; church was not for her. She did it for her grandparents, who were the religious ones. She felt that God had abandoned her long ago.

Had he known who she was right away? He had known by the time she had pulled him onto the dance floor. After one scan of the crowd, she knew it was him. Everybody's eyes had been on her, some swaying to the music, some just letting the music fall on them.

Most of the time, when she had seen him outside the church around town, he looked just like he had tonight. Except tonight he was in jeans, not dark slacks. The button-up shirt had been the same as he usually wore, though tonight's was blue, like his eyes. She had seen him around town looking like that, but never at a raging house party full of drunk college kids.

The slightly curly hair was combed to his head in his preacher hairdo. Later, when she had run her fingers through it, she was not ready for it to go so willingly into the loose curls she had seen hints of over the years. Why he worked so hard to get it to lay flat when the curls made him look so sexy, she'd never know.

Groaning at the memory, she pressed the accelerator harder with her bare foot—she had left her shoes behind. She'd had to get away from him—fast. What would she have done if she had stayed? Probably had sex with the man again. He was good.

She turned the radio on loudly in her pale-yellow Volkswagen beetle, trying to drown out the images in her head, but instead, it just brought her back into his arms, head resting on his hard chest. Once she was encircled in his arms, she felt her fear and worry melt away. He would take care of that, his body said as they swayed to the music.

Of course, her stupid move had been to drag him upstairs to the bedroom. Though she hadn't done something like that since her first few years at college, she wanted to be alone with him. Alone to dance with him without being jostled and bumped into. Just be in his arms and let the music surround them. When they had gotten there, she had been a little sad that she couldn't hear the singer through the floorboards. So, she sang the words so they could still dance.

Wishing she could blame her actions in that bedroom on alcohol, she knew she could not. As far as she knew, two shots of tequila were not enough to seduce a preacher. And she had tasted no alcohol in his mouth when they kissed. God, he was a good kisser.

Turning the radio down, she pulled out her phone, slid through the contacts, and read the names. She wanted to call someone. Talk to someone. Confess what she had done. But none of the names made her hit the call button. The only numbers that appealed to her were those from the book club, but it was so late at night, she knew the book club would wake up and conference call with her about what happened. Over the last half a year, they had gone from near-strangers to the best friends she had. Or maybe just the only friends she had.

Her finger hovered over the call button, unable to press it. She wasn't ready to confess this yet. Was she embarrassed or just not ready to share her memories with Ruston?

Pastor Ruston. If she called the girls, she would have to confess not only that she ran away and attended parties to get away from her life that she always said she loved, but also that she had sex with her minister. Not only hers. Natalie, Mia, and Mandy attended the same church as her. Sometimes they even talked after church, but not often, and not if Mia or Mandy wasn't there. She and Natalie did not talk.

It had been almost six months since the book club had first met. It had started without Hazel. It had started by chance on a Facebook page that Hazel had never heard of but wished she had.

One blustery Saturday afternoon, she had been sitting with her grandparents at the café in downtown Landstad. Mia had been their waitress. But she was the only waitress almost all the time. Though it was her fault since she owned the café and didn't hire extra staff. But it wasn't the waitress who had caught her attention; it was the conversation taking place in the booth behind her.

Tess Thorn from the bank and Ruth Kennedy, who was the secretary at the insurance office just down the road, were talking about a book they were reading, a book about Ted Bundy, the serial killer. Both were in discussion about whether he got away with too much or was credited with too much.

The conversation behind her held more appeal than the one happening in her own booth. Her grandparents were talking about how winter was going to be long, cold, and snowy. It was the same conversation the couple had been having for the last forty-five years they had been married. Hazel had heard it before and a hundred times before and twice that day. Her son beside her was calmly coloring on the kid's menu.

One of her hidden escapes over the past few years had been reading about serial killers. Their crimes and why they do what they do. And now, behind her, two people she knew were talking about one of them openly.

Their conversation dragged on, and Mia dropped off the May family's lunches, then stopped at the booth behind them. Where she told the ladies she too had read the book and hated it. Hazel wished she knew which book they were talking about, but she was unable to look behind her to see without being obvious.

As she ate her hamburger, she heard one of them say, "We are starting a book club, Mia. Are you interested in joining? These are the kinds of books we plan to read and discuss."

Straining to listen, she waited for the bubbly waitress to answer the question, "Yes, where and when?"

One of the others in the booth stated, "We were thinking a weeknight and trade-off places each time."

Mia didn't answer as a customer came in and called out a greeting. Then she answered, "How about Sunday afternoons here? I close at around one pm and have the place cleaned by three. Would that work for you two?"

Both seemed to be in agreement, and Mia walked away to take

another order. Once the waitress was gone, both women started to gather their coats, hats, and mittens. Hazel put down her burger and jumped to her feet, mumbling something to her grandparents about the restroom, and walked down the aisle. As she did, she looked into the booth the women shared to see what book was being read. Recognizing the title, she turned back to look in front of her but too late—she ran into someone who had been walking toward her. Pastor Ruston grabbed her by the shoulders. He was all black coat, dark pants, and steamy blue eyes. Smiling at her, he said, "Excuse me, Hazel." Then he let her go.

The whole incident had been such an embarrassment, she had stayed in the bathroom a little too long. She always had a way of having situations blow up on her. When she had finally made it out of the restroom, he was seated at the booth across from her grandparents, and they were chatting, probably about the weather. The two women were gone, and Mia was talking animatedly to another customer about something.

It had been on the way back to the table that she had noticed Natalie Beckett sitting two tables down from her grandparents. Except for church, Hazel never saw Natalie Beckett; the two did not run in the same circles. Not anymore.

Just seeing her around town made Hazel depressed, and sometimes she would almost hyperventilate. It wasn't Natalie herself that caused the reaction; it was just the fact that she was here. She was alive, and they were gone.

Making it to the booth, she slid in next to her son and pulled him to her, silently praying for his safety, as if danger was close at hand. His struggles made her let him go. He was three and didn't like mom hugs like he used to. Pushing her plate away, she looked at her grandparents, who were looking at her with concern in their eyes. Biting her lip, she excused herself to go sit in the car and wait for them to finish. She'd had enough of people. Neither argued with her about leaving.

As she got up from the booth, her eyes caught Pastor Ruston's, who was studying her like a bug under a microscope. Pulling her eyes away, she walked out into the blowing cold and sat in the car in the parking lot. She had forgotten her coat, but the cold didn't bother her. The cold reminded her she was alive.

To get her mind off her memories of the past that Natalie Beckett always brought up, she pulled out her phone and researched the book the book club was reading. By the time her grandparents made it out of the restaurant with her son and her coat, she had started chapter two of the book. She continued reading as they drove away from the restaurant.

Once home, she put John Henry down for a nap and finished the book, then started another on the same topic. Maybe she could get her grandmother to watch the baby while she would see if others could join the book club, or was it just for professionals from downtown?

In reality, she knew none of the women who would be there. Tess Thorn was the bank president and well over a decade older than Hazel. Both Mia and Ruth were in nearly the same class at school but were around seven years older, and they were all professionals or business owners from downtown. She was just a small-town farmer, and not even a good one.

The next day, it had taken every ounce of courage she had to walk into that café. Way more than getting on stage at a raging party to sing a few songs. None of the four women, expanded to include the nurse practitioner Mandy, had said anything to the younger woman who asked if anyone could join the club. Everyone had smiled, and Mia had jumped up to get another coffee for her.

Sitting with these women who had accomplished so much in life had intimidated Hazel. Even when they asked her a question, she had a hard time answering. Her opinion meant nothing compared to these four.

Pushing her coffee away, she decided she would not be able to do this. Hazel May was not going to be able to let herself enjoy a book club that seemed like just what she needed. Before she could slide out of the booth, Mia sat down next to her, blocking her in. She possibly sensed Hazel was about to leave.

"How about we start with introductions?" Mia said. She was always so upbeat. "I'm Mia. I work and own this place, have for a few years now. I'm single and hate snow and this little town, but I stay because this is where everybody is. My favorite serial killer is not Ted Bundy, but I cannot decide who it is. Angel?"

Ruth Kennedy from the insurance company frowned at Mia and said, "Ruth, just Ruth, Mia. I work at the insurance office a few doors down. Also single, I live above the insurance office and spend almost every weekend with my mom, but it snowed this weekend, so I was able to stick to town. Favorite killer is Dean Carrol. I don't know why. So many details are unknown."

Next to Ruth, Mandy went next, "Mandy Nordskov, nurse at the clinic. Divorced, and new to town, but I did grow up here. Mia is my cousin and invited me. I can read anything about Jack the Ripper."

Tess Thorn glanced at Hazel but realized she wasn't going to say anything. "Tess Thorn, bank president. I'm not from here—I grew up in Minnesota. I really like this little town, very friendly so far. Favorite is The Chessboard Killer if we can choose foreign ones."

Mia's eyes lit up. "That's a good one." Then she turned to Hazel. "Hazel, you're next."

Swallowing hard, she mumbled, "Hazel May, farmer. I have a three-year-old son. I guess I like H. H. Holmes, but I don't know if he actually did many of the murders he was accused of."

"Why not?" Tess was immediately interested. She didn't seem to care that Hazel didn't belong amongst the group.

"Just seems like too much work when nobody really cared at the time how people died. He could have just thrown them into the street, and nobody would have connected them to him. It was the times." She felt she was rambling.

"Interesting take on it. I've heard that the house was exaggerated and not as elaborate as they all say it was," Ruth said from her spot in the kitty-corner from Hazel on the outside of the booth.

Warmth flooded Hazel as she realized these women were actually listening to her, paying attention and wanting to hear what she said. Maybe it would be okay after all.

The bell over the door rang as someone entered. Turning, she looked to see who it was. Natalie Beckett. Panic filled her, and she was trapped in the booth. She needed to get out of the room, away from the other woman.

Trying to control her breathing in hopes of not hyperventilating, she felt Mia put her hand on Hazel's thigh and pull her into a hug with the other arm. "It's okay, Hazel. Natalie didn't do anything. You're okay."

Still being held by the bubbly waitress, Hazel tried to let the panic go. Tears filled her eyes, and her hands shook as Mia said to Mandy, "Go in the kitchen. By the flour on the shelf is a bottle of whiskey—and bring glasses."

Once the nurse came back with the requested items, she poured a generous round for everyone. Each took a glass and downed the contents. Then Tess Thorn refilled them, a little fuller this time, and when all the glasses were empty, Mia finally let go of Hazel, who was not shaking as she had been before.

"Well, that was one way to start a book club. Too much emotion for a murder book club, ladies." Tess sat back down, sliding into the booth where she had been sitting before. Then she poured more whiskey into everyone's glass.

"I guess I need to ask," Mia said, "can you two be in a room together? I've seen you two avoid each other for years." Turning to the other two, she added, "Church is a tense place when they both show up."

"Why?" Tess was not from the area and didn't know. She had no way of knowing the history.

"Can I say?" Ruth asked the two women, one in the corner of the booth, downing another glass of whiskey. The other was sitting in the booth across from the booth the four had started in.

"No," Natalie replied, "I can say it. Hazel hates me for good reason. I killed her brother and sister."

"Jesus Christ, Natalie, you did not kill them. You just survived an accident they didn't," Mia protested.

"That's not how Hazel sees it." Natalie looked right at her as if daring her to deny it.

"It's not that you killed them. You got hurt really bad, but you survived," Hazel whispered into her glass.

Mia put an arm around her and said to Tess, "They were not just her brother and sister, Tess, they were triplets. That makes it a bit harder for Hazel."

"So, Natalie, we were talking about H. H. Holmes. Do you know of him?" Ruth tried to bring the conversation back to murder, which was oddly away from death.

"Yes," Natalie said shakily.

"Actually, we weren't introduced. I don't know Natalie," Tess said to the group.

"My name is Natalie, and I work at the library," Natalie told the group, offering far less information than anyone else had provided.

"From what I hear, she's engaged and getting married late this summer," Mia added. She knew everything that happened in Landstad.

"Yes, in July," Natalie agreed.

"Favorite killer?" Ruth winced that she did not add 'serial' to her sentence.

"The Co-ed Killer," she supplied.

Soon the group was talking about the book they were to read. They all had already read it, and most had read more on the same topic. They discussed, agreed, and disagreed about the killer for three hours.

The memory of that day still brought a smile to her face—she had made the best friends she had ever had that day. To this day, they still get together every other weekend to talk about killers and life. But instead of reading one book about a killer and talking about it, Natalie had changed the group into a podcast. They all read a different book, talked about what they learned, and recorded the conversation, jokes, and all. Afterward, they released the recording to the world. They had gained a small following in the months since, but nobody in town knew anything about it. Even family and partners were unaware of what book club really was.

Pulling up to the farmhouse she had been raised in and still lived in with her grandparents and son, she turned the radio down, noticing it had not taken her as long as it should have to get home. She must have been speeding the entire time.

She walked through the grass, damp from dew, to the house. It was unlocked, so she quietly walked up the stairs and took a quick shower to clean off the makeup and settle the spikes she loved to wear out on the town. Still damp, she pulled on a pair of shorts and a T-shirt to sleep in and carried her party clothes to her bedroom. Throwing them in the corner, she turned to check her on her son, who slept soundly in his crib in the corner of their shared room.

There were three other empty rooms on this floor for him to sleep in—one was storage, and the others remained closed—but she needed him close. She needed to know he was safe. Running her hand through his light blond hair, she was happy he stayed asleep. He was her everything.

Climbing into the twin bed she had always slept in, she tried to not think about the man who, with just a touch, had turned her into a wanton slut. Until she was in his arms, she didn't even think he was very attractive. He was just Pastor Ruston. But once he'd touched her, her body craved more of him. And she wanted to touch him everywhere.

With any luck, he would have been so drunk, he wouldn't remember what had happened. How was she going to face him Sunday morning?

CHAPTER 3

RUSTON HAD SPENT the morning trying not to think about Hazel, just like he had spent the previous day. Now here it was, a bright and sunny summer morning, and all he could do was search her out in the crowd. As the time to start services drew near, he decided she was not coming.

If he were in her shoes, he wouldn't show up. Smiling, he thought about the shoes that were right now in his office. He was going to give them back to her.

When he had made it to his parents' home, Thomas had been on the steps waiting for him, acting like it wasn't him who had abandoned Ruston at the party.

"What happened to you, man? I turned around, and you were gone. I thought you had just left, but you weren't here either." Thomas wanted to know.

"You were making out with someone, and then you were gone. I figured you were hooking up, so I left." Ruston sat down next to his best friend, shoes clenched in his arms—no way was he losing them now.

Thomas leaned over and grabbed a shoe from him. "What's this? Not your style, Rusty."

Ruston looked at the shoe still in his hand and smiled. "I maybe stayed a little longer than I said I did."

"What happened?" Thomas was all smiles.

"I don't even really know. Did you hear the singer who sang 'Life in a Northern Town?'" he asked, still looking at the army shoe that was so small compared to his own foot.

"Yeah, she was great. I've never heard that song sung so good." Thomas confirmed what Ruston already knew.

Holding up the shoe to Thomas, he said, "I know her. She's one of my parishioners. I've never heard her sing before."

He looked at the shoe, something else he had never known about her, that she could be a punk rocker when she wanted to be. Not once did she give off that vibe to him over the years. He knew her: just a small-town girl with a son and family who loved her.

"Oh man, you did the whole preacher thing, didn't you? Talked to her about her problems. Did you get her to get back together with her boyfriend?" Thomas wanted to know.

Ruston laughed. Over the years, he seemed to find the girl at a party who just wanted to forget about her ex. What should have turned into an easy lay turned into long talks. Then, after a while, off she would go, making up with the man she had wanted to forget. Ruston was always left wondering how it happened. "Nope, no talking."

His friend looked over at him, handing him the shoe back. "You didn't."

"Unfortunately, we did. I don't even know how it happened. One minute we were dancing, and the next, we were not." Ruston's mind went back to that room and her body against his, her hands touching his, his touching her. He wanted to touch her again.

"And you know her? And she's a part of your flock?" Thomas was all-out laughing at him.

"Yes."

"You fucked your flock?" Thomas said, still laughing.

"Don't talk about her like that, Thomas. There's something about her. I just don't know what to do about it." Ruston had spent the walk there trying to figure it out. He hadn't found the answer to that yet.

"Are you going to date her? She looked pretty young. Hot, but young." Thomas stopped laughing and was now serious.

"I don't think she would date me. I'm surprised she danced with me," Ruston replied, repeating the conclusion he had come to on the walk.

"You're a catch, Rusty. Any woman would love to date you," Thomas tried to reassure him.

"Not Hazel. She's been there since I started. Until today, I've never touched her."

"What do you mean? Touch her? You're not really supposed to touch your flock. I think it's frowned upon." Thomas was trying to understand.

"She's one of those people who you can tell who goes to church because someone makes them—her grandparents in her case. She doesn't listen to my sermons, she doesn't sing songs, she doesn't volunteer for things. Just stares off into space for an hour and goes home. In fact, she doesn't shake my hand at the end of the service." Ruston had noticed all this over the past few months. It had started to bother him just after last Christmas.

It had been then when he had started noticing her more and more. Which was why he knew she didn't pay attention, because he was suddenly paying attention to her every week.

"Why doesn't she shake your hand at the end?" Thomas asked. "Everybody does."

"She always walks between her grandparents and carries her son with two hands and doesn't let go of him. I touch the boy's head and bless him, but she doesn't acknowledge me. No smile, no nothing." In fact, tonight was the first time he had seen a smile from her.

"She had a kid? Is she old enough for a kid?" Thomas leaned back on the door behind them.

"Yeah, he's only like three. I don't know how old she is, but she hadn't been in high school during the time I was there. She farms with her grandpa."

"No baby daddy?" Thomas raised an eyebrow.

"Not that I know of. But then again, I see her on Sunday and maybe once a month around town. Not enough to know a lot about her." Ruston looked at the two shoes in his hand. Right now, he wished he was more into listening to the gossip around town, but then that wasn't him.

"So, you literality knocked the boots off her and then left?" Thomas chuckled.

"No, she left me. I was unable to catch her."

"Do you want to do it again?"

"What?"

"It. With her?" Thomas wiggled an eyebrow at him.

Ruston sighed. "In a heartbeat."

"Because she was so good and it was so hot or because she was Hazel?" Thomas knew the perfect questions. Maybe that was the reason he was a high school counselor.

"Mostly because she's Hazel. She fascinates me. There's something about her. When we were dancing upstairs, we could only hear the music the band was playing, not the words, so she sang the words to us just above a whisper. And a few months ago, I ran into her at a restaurant in town, and she nearly had a panic attack right in the middle of the place and nobody even acknowledged it. Everyone knows something, but I don't know it." Ruston knew he was rambling, but he continued anyway.

"Well, I guess you're going to have to date her then. It's the only way to know," Thomas said from behind him, leaning against the door.

"Know what?"

"Know if you're already in love with her. You have it bad." Thomas pushed Ruston's back.

"I barely know her."

"And you still have it bad, so wait until you know her better." Thomas jumped to his feet. "I have to get home now that I know you're alive. Very alive."

Watching him head to his car, he wondered if Thomas was right.

Should he try to date the blonde woman? Thomas was wrong about being in love with her, but maybe one day.

Looking around one more time, he realized that if he never saw her again, he couldn't fall for her. Their only connection was church, and if she stopped coming, he was out of luck.

Walking to the front of the church, he welcomed everyone as he watched her grandparents walk in through the back door. Smiling for the first time that day, he watched her walk in behind them, carrying her son while wearing a sundress with large yellow flowers. Her hair was lying flat on her head, but it was styled nicely. He knew she was not wearing makeup. Taking their usual seats, she settled the boy on her lap and fussed over him a little as Ruston read the announcements.

For the entire service, he couldn't keep his eyes off her. But she didn't look at him. She was fussing with the boy, keeping him busy and quiet, or she was just starting off in the distance. Once again, she just stood while the rest of the congregation sang. She didn't even pretend to pay attention to the sermon, and when it was time for communion, she did not partake.

Church and religion had such an important place in his life, it hurt that she considered it a waste of time. He wanted it to be more to her than something she put up with for her family.

Shaking hands and greeting his parishioners was usually one of his favorite parts, finding out how everyone was, but today he just wanted to get through them as he waited for the May family to make it through the line. Twelve more people. Six more people. One more person, and there they were.

"Morning, Rose. How are you doing?" He shook her hand, smiling at the older woman who really looked nothing like her young grand-daughter.

"Good. It's a busy time now for John and Hazel," Rose commented.

"Hopefully, you let them cut loose sometimes, Rose." He teased her, but his eyes were on the hazel ones behind her. No smile, no acknowl-edgment, nothing.

Rose walked away, and he turned to Hazel, who was holding tight to her small son. Oddly, the boy's hazel eyes smiled at Ruston. Touching the soft blond hair so much like his mother's, he said, "Bless you, John." Then he turned to his mother and also touched her head in the same manner, making her eyes meet his for the first time. "I want to talk to you, Hazel." Not waiting for her to answer, he held out his hand to her grandfather, who shook it in greeting.

Trying to quickly to get through the remaining parishioners, he said good morning to the last one and headed down to find Hazel. Would she have waited for him? Searching the familiar faces, he didn't see her or her grandparents. Turning, he looked out the window to the parking lot and saw her little yellow beetle driving out of the lot.

She was gone.

Again.

CHAPTER 4

PULLING off the headphones that Natalie insisted they wear when recording, Hazel laughed at the story Tess had started as soon as 'stop' was pushed on the recording. Tess had a way of making life far more fun than it actually was. Though she worked as president of the only bank in town, she was always telling stories of her childhood in a large family. Today it was about a small flock of sheep she and her sister had hidden from their father in their bedroom.

When Hazel had first met the women, they'd seemed so intimidating, but now they were just her friends who happened to have cool jobs. They were fun to hang around with, and she looked forward to their biweekly get-together. They seemed to accept her as one of them.

Today she was exceptionally happy to be there because she had forced herself to go to church this morning so her grandmother would let her off that afternoon. If she had told the older woman she was too sick to attend services, she would also have to be too sick to go out with her friends. So, she forced herself to sit and watch Pastor Ruston, trying not to remember how he had yelled swear words when he came. She also tried not to remember his hands on her body or how it felt as his cock slipped through her lips. For the entire hour, she had not been able to look at his face.

Was he thinking about her?

Having made it through the service, all she had needed to do was to get through the greeting line without looking at him. She actually enjoyed when he touched her son's head, acknowledging the boy every Sunday. But then he had run a hand over her head as he had John Henry's. He had never done that before. She thought he had accepted that she wouldn't shake his hand at the end of the service, but today, he touched her. She thought he was going to bless her as well, but in the end, he just wanted to talk to her. Of course, he did. But there was no way she was talking to him. They just had to put that night behind them and move on. Forget, forget, forget.

As her eyes caught his bright blue ones, she couldn't say a word. Her voice was lost in the pools of bright blue that made her remember every second of their night together. Night? It wasn't even an hour. Instantly, she wanted another hour with him.

Someone said her name, pulling her back from the memory of his eyes. "Earth to Haze," Ruth said from the chair beside her. The group had started calling her by her childhood nickname almost imme-diately.

"What's on your mind tonight?" Tess had poured herself another drink as she sat back at the table.

"Nothing. Just letting my mind go, that's all," she lied. Then distracted, she asked, "How is the wedding coming, Natalie?"

"Good, it's less than a week away," Natalie admitted, not exactly acting excited about the short timeframe.

"When does Jason come to town?" Mandy asked. Jason was Natalie's fiancé, but he lived in Fargo, over three hours away. Once the wedding was over, she would be leaving them to make a life with him in the big city. Hazel didn't think she was excited about leaving—her dad was here, and she had a good job at the library.

Hazel was a little jealous of her. Not for getting to leave, but for having a job. It was a career, actually. Though Hazel had been farming for a few years now, she always felt it was neither a job nor a career. Just what she did.

"Thursday night, maybe Friday morning depending on his mood," she informed the group, her usual smile absent. "Are you guys coming to the rehearsal dinner on Friday night?"

Natalie had invited them to the dinner since the wedding part was small and her family was just her and her dad. The book club would fill an empty space in the church basement. Only Mia was actually in the wedding as her personal attendant; the rest were just guests.

Everyone agreed they would be there, though Hazel didn't know if she could leave her son with her grandparents for two days in a row. The wedding was probably more important, so she was planning to attend that. Knowing that if she voiced it to the rest, they would talk her into going to both. But she hated to leave John Henry with the older couple too much. So far, they had raised their only daughter and three grand-children, they didn't need to raise her son too. She would be doing that.

Natalie was watching her for some reason. Did she know Hazel wasn't going to the dinner at the end of the week? Was she on to her plans? If anyone could read her mind, it would be Natalie. "Hazel, can I talk to you in the living room?"

Hazel nodded but hesitated before she got up. Draining her remaining wine, she followed her dark-haired former classmate into the room next to the kitchen. The other four watched them go with puzzled expressions. Hazel shot them a matching expression as she followed.

Watching Natalie's back, Hazel couldn't remember a day in her life when Natalie wasn't taller than her. Since the first day of kinder-garten, Natalie was tall, dark, and different, which was why she had excelled in sports.

Natalie had sat in a side chair and had put her glass of wine on the coffee table. Hazel sat on the end of couch close to the other woman. Had she noticed something at church? Natalie had been there this morning. Had everyone heard what had happened? Did Ruston talk about it? Did everyone know? What would happen if everyone knew?

Panic rose, and she started to concentrate on her breathing. Slow and steady. Breathe in, breathe out. With effort, she didn't put her head between her knees as she had been instructed years ago when the attacks started, back when they were happening every day.

Natalie was looking at her and put her hand on Hazel's knee to calm her. "Hazel, what's the matter?"

"Nothing," Hazel lied.

"I was just going to ask if you wanted to learn the program for the podcast so that you can do it while I'm on my honeymoon," Natalie explained, still touching her leg. "What did you think I wanted to talk to you about?"

"Nothing." Hazel rubbed her eyes with the palms of her hands, trying to get her emotions under control.

"Are you coming to my wedding?" she asked.

"Yes," was all she said. Right now, she didn't know if she would go to any of it. Not if this might happen.

"Good, I'm glad we've become friends again, Haze." Natalie grinned as she patted her friend's leg.

"We were never friends before." Hazel bit her lip at the slip-up. The past was supposed to be in the past.

"Before the accident, we were. We always hung out together when we were young. You, me, and Hanna." Natalie's voice cracked a little as she said the last name, a name that hadn't been said between them in the months they had gotten together. Not once. But it hung above them just the same.

"No, you and Hanna were friends. You just put up with me because I was there. You two were the friends, best friends," Hazel replied, trying not to cry. "Then when we got older, Henry joined in, but I stopped going with. I didn't really feel welcomed into your group. Not anymore."

Natalie now had tears running down her cheeks. "You were always welcome. You were the one who didn't want to do things with us anymore."

"I wasn't invited anymore. Hanna said I was boring and brought everyone down because I wasn't all that fun," Hazel admitted about her identical twin. She hated talking about the bad things in her character.

"It wasn't me who didn't want you along. I missed you. You changed that last year you weren't around as much," Natalie admitted.

"I was wasting time on music; that's what they always said. A waste of time. When they died, I stopped. That's what it took for me to stop," Hazel said through her tears. She had never told anyone why she had stopped singing, but now it was out.

"You were really good, Hazel. You shouldn't have stopped. They wouldn't have wanted you to stop."

"I had to. My dreams were nothing compared to theirs. I need their dreams to be fulfilled. That's what I'm doing." Why was she telling Natalie her secrets? Natalie didn't care. She had never cared about Hazel. Hanna had been her friend, after all.

"But those were their dreams, and they had to die with them. You need to be you, Hazel. That's what has been missing all these years. *You*." Natalie tried to grab her hand, but Hazel pulled away, so she couldn't get it.

"Their dreams are the only thing I have now. They are dead. I should have died that day too." She ran out of the apartment.

If Natalie followed, she didn't know. All she knew was that she needed to get out of here. The tears were running down her face as she ran down the stairs from Ruth's apartment. Pushing the outside door open, she rushed to her car sitting just down the street.

It was just after seven on a Sunday night on Main Street. There were never other people around when book club broke up. Landstad had definitely closed down for the night.

She couldn't see through her tears as she ran toward her car. Pulling her keys from her pocket, she just had to get into the car. Needed to get as far from Natalie and everyone else as she could, as fast as she could. If she could leave her thoughts behind, she would.

Before she could step off the curb, someone grabbed her around the waist. She wished she had no idea who it was, but her body screamed his name, remembering the feel of his hands on her. His mouth. Ruston.

"Let me go!" She hated yelling at him, but she needed to leave, to get as far from there as possible.

"No way you are driving like this. You'll get yourself killed and maybe someone else," Ruston said into her hair as he held on to her, maybe even tightening his grip on her.

"Would that be so bad?" she whispered frantically.

"Yes, Hazel, it would be. Think about John. What would happen to him if his mom died?" Ruston brought out the big guns. Her son was the most important thing to her. Hell, he was the only important thing to her.

Her head went into her hands as she cried in his arms. Her body shook from the tears that she was unable to stop. The guilt that was always present was now pounding into her head. She should be dead, not them. They had so much more going for them than her. Why did they both die at seventeen, while she still lived on? Why was she allowed to live? They had all been born on the same day, so they should have died the same day. It was only fair.

As the guilt rolled over her, she suddenly couldn't breathe, couldn't catch her breath. Gasping for air, she knew in her mind she was having a panic attack, but she couldn't remember anything about how to stop it. She couldn't remember how to breathe!

Being in Ruston's arms was calming, but not enough to make her emotions go away. She wanted him to dance with her but couldn't get the words out. Just sway in his arms until the hurt disappeared. He had to be able to make the hurt stop. He was Ruston.

Trying to catch her breath, she heard her friends around her. Someone shoved a bag over her mouth so that she was breathing in and out of the bag. Ruston still held her tight.

When her mind stopped spinning with thoughts and visions of Henry and Hanna and their ultimate deaths, she could finally make sense of the scene around her. Ruston was still holding her tight, and she was still breathing into a bag that Mandy was holding up for her, since her arms were being held tight to her body. Mia, Tess, and Ruth were standing around, watching the scene. Their faces showed concern for their young friend. Natalie was not around, or maybe she was, and Hazel couldn't see her. She didn't know which.

Waving the lower part of her arms, she pulled away from the bag. "I'm okay now." Mandy lowered the bag, but Ruston kept a hold of her. Which was for the best since she didn't know if her legs worked anymore.

"What happened?" Mia asked. "What did Natalie say?"

"Nothing, it was me. I don't know." The answer didn't make sense to her either.

"Can you stand, Hazel?" Mandy asked since Ruston was still holding her.

"Yes, I think so." Ruston lowered her to the ground, and she realized he had lifted her up.

"Are you okay?" Ruston pressed, but about standing or in general, she didn't know.

"Yes." She swayed a little and then stood tall.

Mia took her hand. "I'm taking Hazel home. She cannot drive like this, and it'll just upset Rose and probably John Henry."

Hazel had no reply to that. She was exhausted and had no energy to argue, though she had wanted it to be Ruston who was bringing her home. There was no energy to argue against her feelings for him. She just wanted to be held in his arms for longer.

Hazel was unable to say anything as the girls left Ruston on the street and ushered her across the road and up into Mia's apartment. Once inside, she left them and went to the bathroom to see what she looked like. And she looked as bad as she had thought that she would. Good thing she didn't go with Ruston.

By the time she got herself together enough to leave the bathroom, everyone but Mia had left, which was for the best. he didn't want so many people around, even if they were only there to help.

With trepidation, she called her grandmother. Hazel never knew if her grandmother would be happy to watch her son for longer or demanded she came home. She was relieved when she was happy to let her stay in town overnight. John Henry was already asleep. Just having too much fun with friends, she had told the older lady, which caused her grandma to remind her to be home before her son woke up in the morning. Mia had loaned her something to sleep in, and she had just climbed into the spare bed when Mia came into the room with a glass of water.

Setting it on the bedside table, Mia sat down on the bed. "Are you really okay?

Hazel laid her head on the pillow and said, "Physically, yes. I'm fine. Emotionally, I'm not going to survive."

"Have you ever seen anyone about the panic attacks?" Mia asked.

"No. Just no." Hazel rolled to look at the woman sitting beside her. "It won't help. I cannot be helped, Mia."

"I want to help, Haze. I want you to be better. I know what happened that day, and I don't know how you survived it. Sometimes I think your injuries were worse than Natalie's. All she had to do was heal on the outside, and she had all kinds of help with that from doctors and specialists. Your injuries were hidden, and nobody was there for you. I see you at church, but you don't participate." Mia ran her fingers over Hazel's short blonde hair.

"God and I don't talk. I just go for Grandma. She wants me there."

"Do you think you could talk to Pastor Ruston? He was a great help tonight. I could tell he relaxed you during the panic attack," Mia replied.

"No, I can't go to him." Hazel rolled back onto her back away from Mia's eyes.

"He's really good at counseling. I've heard of a lot of people who have gone to him. They've had good results," Mia pushed.

"No, Mia," Hazel warned.

"Maybe if you could just listen to him talk and look at his cute face. Do you think he's ripped?" Mia questioned.

"Yes," Hazel whispered as the memory of his chest under her roaming fingers came to mind.

"Have you seen him with his shirt off?" Mia was all interested suddenly.

"No, nothing like that." True, Hazel had never seen him without his shirt on. "Can we drop it?"

"I really don't want too, Haze. What happened? You don't have to tell if you don't want to." Mia scooted closer to Hazel, lying on the other side of the bed.

"Mia," Hazel warned.

"Come on, Hazel, girl talk. Please," Mia begged.

"What do you want to know?" Hazel was already regretting it. Sex with Ruston was her memory. She really didn't want to share it.

"Was it an accident?" Mia started to drink the water Hazel was sure that Mia had brought for her.

"What?" Hazel wondered. It was all an accident; none of it was an accident.

"Rephrase." Mia sighed in exasperation. "Did you accidentally feel his chest or was that on purpose?"

"Purpose." Hazel smiled at the memory of her hands running up his chest then down again.

"Were you on a date?" Mia prodded.

"No," was all Hazel said.

"Was it a long time ago?" Mia pressed on.

"No." Hazel rolled her eyes.

"So recently you were not on a date but felt his chest, but did not get to see it," Mia pieced together.

"Yes," Hazel agreed.

"Have you kissed him? Him, you know, the preacher." Mia was having a good time with the interrogation.

"Yes."

"Tongue or no tongue?"

"Definitely tongue." Hazel smiled at the memory.

"Is he good?" Mia asked.

"Oh yeah, he is good," Hazel replied, still smiling.

"Wait, I meant is he a good kisser, but you make it sound like more. How many bases did you get to, Hazel May?" Mia demanded, eyes wide.

"It was a home run." Hazel laughed out loud at Mia's expression of complete shock.

"What? He's not supposed to be scoring runs! He's a pastor!" Mia flopped on her back next to Hazel.

"He's not a priest; he's a single guy. It really wasn't planned, and I don't think he wanted to do it. It just happened pretty fast, and he went with the flow." Hazel had analyzed why he went through with it for the last few days. After all, it was all she could think about.

"Are you planning on dating him?" Mia asked the ceiling.

"No, he can't date me," Hazel said.

"Can't or won't?" Mia asked, looking over at her.

"I don't think he wants to, and he can't anyway."

"Why can't he?" You're over twenty, a single lady, and you attend his church. Might be a perfect match," Mia pointed out.

"I'm a bastard with a bastard son. He's a minister." At least she assumed her mother never married her father. Hazel had actually never seen the woman. Her grandparents had taken the three babies home from the hospital, and her mother had gone back to the world of drugs she enjoyed more than her family, never coming back or getting in contact.

"Nobody cares about that anymore, Hazel," Mia argued.

"Yes, they do. I'm treated differently than other moms. You don't see it because it isn't happening to you. I've not been asked to join the ladies club at church, but I bet you have," Hazel pointed out.

"Maybe I have, but I have not joined," Mia defended herself, not that Hazel could see Mia leading any church group.

"Beyond that, he won't date me anyway," Hazel said.

"Oh, I think he would. I saw his face tonight." Mia sat up.

"He would probably date me for a little bit, but then it would end. We don't have a lot in common." Hazel had come to that conclusion during church that morning.

"Do I have to start listing all the things you have in common again?" Mia said.

"Any relationship will end between us because I don't believe in his God. He won't be able to accept that." It was the reason nothing would ever work between them, no matter how good he was in bed.

"But you go to church every week," Mia argued, sitting up again.

"For my grandma. She wants me there. But the God who took my family away doesn't get my attention." She turned away from her friend and curled into a ball.

Mia was silent for a while, then got up to leave. Quietly, she shut the light off, and Hazel said, "Please don't tell anyone about Ruston and me. He doesn't need that getting around. I will not be the reason his job could be in jeopardy."

As she lay in the darkness in a tight ball, she let the tears run down her face as she cried for the relationship that never had a chance. For the man whose touch could calm her and turn her on at the same time. For the future that always feels just out of reach. Then for the past that she couldn't change.

CHAPTER 5

FRIDAY HAD BEEN a long day waiting for the wedding rehearsal. He was pretty sure Hazel would be in attendance tonight—full meal and a full bar could draw just about anyone. After spending an hour mingling with the attendees, all the while searching for her blonde pixie cut, he gave up. She was a no-show. If he could leave, he would.

Once the meal had started, he noticed that her book club was having the most fun at this get-together. Even the bride, who sat next to the groom at the head table, looked bored and wished she could join her friends.

The ladies laughed loudly again and drew the eyes of the wedding party before they started to shush themselves again. At least someone was having a good time.

Taking another drink of his pop, he turned to the bride's father, who he was seated next to. "Are you excited for the wedding tomorrow?"

"Truth?" the father, Patrick Beckett asked quietly. "Not really. It's been just Natalie and me since her mom passed away when she was six. I don't know how to feel about letting someone else into our family."

"You never thought of remarrying?" Ruston asked. He knew Natalie was twenty-three, and for seventeen years, he had been alone.

"Once, but life got in the way. Since then, it just never really got there again." He looked down the table at the woman who had spent months creating the flowers for the wedding.

"Faith? Since when?" They always sat together at church, but he assumed it was because they were neighbors and friends.

"Oh, close to ten years now," the older man admitted a little sheepishly.

"And you never thought about marrying her?"

"Oh yes, many times. First, Natalie wasn't ready, then there was the accident and recovery. Then it just got lost in life. We're comfortable with it now."

"What accident?" Ruston had never heard of Patrick being in an accident.

"The accident," was all Patrick said. At Ruston's puzzled look, he added, "When Natalie was seventeen, she was in a major car accident. One car rollover. The driver had been drinking; they all had. Natalie spent almost a year in Fargo recovering. Many surgeries. We thought we had lost her many times. She only had a twenty-five percent chance of survival that first week. I really never thought I would see this day."

"Wow." Ruston had never heard of it. Even if it had happened years before he had moved to town, he would have thought it would have come up.

"Yeah, a lot of people don't talk about it. It was a heavy blow to the community. Four kids didn't graduate that year. Three were dead." Patrick looked out at the crowd of kids who might have been there, who might have been affected by it.

"When did it happen?" He didn't want to know why he was so interested, but he was.

"November fifth. I will never forget that day." Patrick watched his daughter eating in the distance. She must have felt his eyes on her because she smiled at him.

Once eating had ended, the rehearsal started. Making sure everyone knew what to do and when to do it. The book club sat in the back of the pews, heads together, chatting and laughing.

With everyone knowing what to do, he dismissed them, and the bridesmaids and groomsmen cheered and took off. That left the bride and groom alone at the altar with Ruston. Natalie turned to her groom and said, "Jason, I need to talk to Pastor Ruston."

The groom just nodded and walked away to his friends. Ruston took a breath and asked, "Do you want to talk here or in my office?"

"Office." She glanced over her shoulder. He saw the book club looking at them, whispering to each other before he turned and led her to his office.

Walking in, he led her into the room and then closed the door behind them. "What can I do for you, Natalie?"

She sat down in a chair. "It's about Sunday night. I feel bad about what happened with Hazel."

"What happened with Hazel?" He knew he shouldn't pry, but he did. He wanted to know what had caused her so much distress.

"I really don't know. We were talking, and I guess the conversation turned to growing up together. Then the conversation turned again, and I could see and hear her going deep into herself. I think she carries around so much guilt, too much guilt. Some of it should be on me." She went silent and looked down at her hands.

"Does she do it a lot? Go deep, as you say?" He sat down on the corner of his desk.

"I don't know," Natalie admitted. "We've only been friends for the last few months again. Before that, we couldn't be in the same room without her having a panic attack. For years. I feel bad about it, but I can't do anything about it."

"What changed and made you friends again?" he asked.

"Book club. We get along when we're in a group. But alone, we have guilt issues."

"Guilt about what?" He needed to know because Natalie needed his help—not because it was about Hazel.

"The accident," Natalie whispered.

"Guilt about what? She wasn't the one in the car." He knew all the others in the car except for Natalie had died. Patrick had said as much just a few hours before.

"I think she wishes she had been." Tears started to run down her cheeks, so he handed her some tissue.

"That makes sense with that she said when I stopped her from driving that night. Do you think she would do anything about it?" Ruston wanted to run out of the room, the building, and hunt the woman down. Hold her in his arms until he knew she was safe.

"I don't know. She has John Henry, and only her grandparents are left to take care of him. I know she would never let them raise another child. They already raised her and her siblings." Natalie wiped her eyes.

Who were they? He had never seen anyone with them at church. Not even on holidays.

"I will try and talk to her after the wedding. I've been trying for a week now and have been unsuccessful, but I will work harder on it. If I have no luck, I might have to have you help when you get back from your honeymoon." Ruston tried to lighten the mood. He couldn't tell if he had been successful or not when she walked out the door.

Getting up and walking around to his desk chair, he sunk down. What was happening to the short blonde who was always on his mind? Would she come to the wedding or blow that off too?

A shiver of fear ran down his spine when he remembered her face coming toward him Sunday night. He had been out for a walk and noticed her little yellow car parked on Main Street and, deciding it was time to talk, leaned against the car to wait. Having waited for over an hour, he was about to give up when she slammed out of the door. Rushing toward her car, he knew she didn't see him, that she didn't see anything.

He grabbed her around the waist. He had no idea what was happening with her, just that he was not letting her go. When she had said she would be better off dead, the hair on the back of his neck stood up. He had heard suicide threats before, but this was the first one that felt completely real. And it scared him to death.

When the five women poured out of the building, he knew he couldn't let her go, and they didn't push him to. Her sobs were tearing his heart out right there on Main Street. What had happened to her that her body could shake with sobs until she struggled to breathe?

Mandy had been prepared with a paper bag.

Ruth had muttered something about panic attacks, the same type she had almost suffered from in the restaurant. It seemed people in this town were aware of her attacks, and nobody seemed to care enough to try and get them to stop. Just let them happen to the poor woman.

Mia had taken charge and taken Hazel to her place before Ruston could come up with a reason to take her home with him. All he wanted was to hold her in his arms until she was happy again. Until she knew someone cared about her. Until she knew he cared about her.

Pulling out his phone from his pocket, he wanted to text her to see if she was okay, but he didn't know her number. Or even if she had a phone.

Putting his phone down, he got up to see if everyone was gone. Walking through the empty church, he stopped at a framed picture of confirmation classes hanging on the wall. He found the picture he wanted and pulled the small class of seven off the wall, looking closely at the girl in the back row with long brown hair. She had a cocky smile and a name he recognized, but a face he had never seen before. Her nose and chin were different. Her eyes were the green he recognized, but her smile was different than the one she had given her father over supper. Extensive surgery, Patrick had said, and it seemed it was.

Scanning the picture for other familiar faces, he found one he was not expecting, but then again, he was. He knew Natalie and Hazel were the same age. Finding her standing next to Natalie, she had long blonde hair back then, swept back into a clip on her head. Her hazel eyes had a mischievousness about them. That was gone now. Smiling, his eyes slid to see her name in block letters right after Natalie's, and his heart stopped. It said Hanna May, not Hazel. Quickly, he scanned the rest of the names, passing over faces he didn't recognize. At the end, in the front row, he found Hazel May printed in block letters. His eyes lifted to a carbon copy of the first girl he had thought was Hazel. Eyes darting from one to the other and back again, he whispered, "Twins."

"Identical," a voice said behind him, making him jump. Mia was leaning against the wall. "Hanna and Hazel were identical. Henry is in there too. He made the three."

His eyes scanned the picture and found the tall young man in the back row, right behind Hazel. "Where are they?"

"Dead. They always call it Natalie's accident. But really it should be called the May's accident. She lost both of them that day. The three became one in an instant. She changed that day. The Hazel who sang her heart out in the choir and just for fun was gone. I haven't heard her sing since that day. Nobody has." Mia looked at the picture in his hand.

"I didn't know," he told her, still looking at the picture.

"If you really like her, you should know. She's had a lot of pain in her lifetime, and most of it she hasn't let go of yet. If you really want her, you will have to work for her." Mia was still leaning against the wall.

"Who said I like her?" Ruston questioned.

Smirking, she shrugged. "She likes you too, but you'll have to help her over the pain before you can have a future together."

"I don't know if I want a future with her, Mia," Ruston admitted.

"You wouldn't have had sex with her if you hadn't thought there was a future, Pastor Ruston. Don't lie to yourself about that." Mia pushed herself from the wall.

"My friend said that I was already in love with her."

"There are a lot of obstacles to get over before it can be love, Ruston. But it could happen if you're up for the challenge." She turned and walked out of the church.

When he heard the door slam behind her, he looked back at the picture in his hand. Finding her easily this time, he stared at her hazel eyes, so happy and without the constant pain he saw in them now. He wished he could have met that young, carefree girl who loved to sing. But maybe it was fate that he had met her at a house party where he was able to hold her in his arms as she sang the songs they danced to.

What if he wasn't able to get over the obstacles of her past? What if it was more than he could overcome?

CHAPTER 6

FANNING herself with the wedding program, Hazel waited for the hottest wedding ever to start so it could get done and she could get out of this stuffy church. How it could be raining so hard outside and still be a steam bath in the church? If she didn't know better, she would think Satan himself was invited to the wedding.

The church was full, and she hadn't gotten there in time to get a seat with anyone from the book club. Mandy, Tess, and her boyfriend Math were close to the front. Ruth and her boyfriend Anderson were sitting in the back on the other side of the aisle from her.

John Henry wiggled on her lap, and she handed the program to him so he could play with it. Her fan was a crumpled mess in moments. Originally, she had planned on leaving him at home with her grandma, but both of her grandparents looked tired that day, so she decided to just take the little guy.

Hugging him to her, she could feel the heat of his little body against hers, even in the blistering church. She was glad she had put on a white jean skirt and a thin pale pink blouse, but she wished she could have worn less. But anything less wouldn't be appropriate for public.

Picking up her phone, she hit a button to see the time. Five minutes late. Maybe Mia wasn't doing a good job as Natalie's personal attendant. Hazel knew it took more than one woman to keep Natalie on track. An army would be challenged. Her phone was still in her hand when it buzzed.

Mia: Basement, now!!!

Sliding out of the pew carrying John Henry, she saw that Mandy and Tess were walking her way. When they made it out of the sanctuary, Ruth had joined them. All four women and one little boy walked into the basement, which was twenty degrees colder than upstairs. Sweet cold air.

Tess pushed her way past the three bridesmaids sitting at tables waiting for the wedding to start. They'll be happy they got a few more moments in the cool basement air, Hazel decided.

When all three were in the room with Mia, she slammed the door closed. "Natalie is gone."

"Gone where?" Mandy asked.

"Let's just say gone and done with this situation," Mia replied.

"She bolted?" Hazel asked in surprise. For months the woman had been looking forward to nothing but this moment. And now she had left before it started?

"Yes. I sent her off in my car. I need a ride from someone." Mia was still sitting on the table, calm as can be. As if a church full of people wasn't above them waiting for the bride—a now missing bride.

"How did she get out past the bridesmaids?" Ruth asked.

"Out the window." Mia pointed at a tiny window in the back of the room.

Tess shook her head as she analyzed the window.

"Now what?" Ruth asked.

"We have to wait about twenty minutes. I told her I would give her time. Then we tell her dad and Ruston." Mia had been planning this, apparently.

All four stood silently for a few minutes, looking out the window at the rain pounding the ground near the window.

"Why are there no chairs in this room?" Ruth demanded, and all four of them erupted into fits of laughter. Even John Henry joined in with belly laughs of his own.

The laughter stopped abruptly when there came a knock on the door. Everyone looked at the door and held their breaths. A knock came again. "Natalie, are you ready? I want to talk to you." It was her dad.

Mandy jumped and opened the door a crack, then pulled the middle-aged man into the room with the five women, slamming the door shut again behind him.

"Where's Natalie?" The man looked around the room as if his kid could hide her white dress and tall frame among these women.

"She left," Mia answered simply.

"When?" he asked.

"About ten minutes ago. I promised to give her twenty," Mia shyly told the older man.

All eyes were on the man who had spent a lot of money on this get together. "I guess we have ten minutes to wait then."

All the women started to breathe again.

"Okay, Mandy, Tess, and Ruth, go back and sit down. Look natural and wait for the announcement. Haze, I need you to tell Ruston what's happening. You will have to go outside and go in the back way to the room behind the alter. He will need to know what's happening, that the wedding is off." Mia gave out orders to everyone.

"Why me? I can't take the baby with me." As the others left the room, she looked out the window at the rain pouring down still.

"Because nobody will notice that you didn't come back. They'll just think the baby needed out of there. Nobody will think anything of it. Mr. Beckett, your jacket, please." Mia took the jacket Natalie's father had instantly taken off without question. Then she threw it on over John Henry's head. Then pulled it off again, making the boy giggle. "You have to go out the window."

"I will not, I'm wearing a white skirt. *White.*" She looked at the little window. If Natalie had made it out, she knew she could. But did she want to?

"For Natalie," Mia said, as if she owed anything to the woman. Years of friendship meant she couldn't *not* do it, even if it meant getting wet and dirty.

"Fine. When I am out, send him out with the jacket on him." She climbed onto the table in front of the window. Sighing, she opened the window and felt cool, wet air on her face. Then, with no grace at all, she slid out the window onto the wet grass. She was completely dirty and wet in seconds.

John Henry was sent carefully out the window by Patrick Beckett himself. Pulling him into her arms, she ran up the stairs behind the church and hoped that it was actually unlocked. Prayers answered, she opened the door and threw herself into the little room, then kicked the door closed. As if the rain chased her.

As far back as she could remember, the room had held the communion wine, a big draw for her brother and sister in their teens.

"Hazel, what are you doing here?" Ruston squatted down and pulled the jacket off John Henry's head. The boy smiled at the preacher and said, "Peekaboo."

She watched his blue eyes light up and answered back to her little boy, "Peekaboo to you, too." Then he turned his blue eyes on her. "Hazel?"

"Natalie bolted. We're stalling for time so that she can get out of here," Hazel revealed in a rush, wondering if she needed to explain it better. But what more was there?

"Okay, what's the plan?" With a nod, he got to his feet and pulled her to hers.

"That is the plan. I don't know anything beyond that," Hazel hissed at him. How much planning did he think went into this? The bride was gone, and the wedding was off. That was everything.

All he did was smile at her, which made her a little madder. With ease, he lifted the boy from her hip and moved him to his. John Henry said nothing as a strange man took him from his mother. The boy pulled back a little and looked at Ruston's face, then leaned into him, raising his hand to Ruston's almost curly hair and said, "Bless you."

Ruston's blue eyes lit up with laughter at the little boy and then turned those laughing eyes on her. She couldn't stop the smile on her lips if she tried.

With his free hand, he touched her cheek as she smiled at him. "You have a dimple. I've never seen it before. Then his lips lowered and touched hers lightly. It was nothing more than a chaste kiss. A light kiss and his breath on her face, but it made her want more. Way more.

Behind them, the gentle music stopped playing. Ruston seemed reluctant as he pulled away and headed out to the sanctuary. It was time for him to inform everyone that the wedding was off.

"Ruston," she called, and he stopped to look at her in question. "You can't take John Henry with you. It would look weird."

He smiled at her as he handed her back the boy. "You stay in here for a while. Your shirt is wet and is now see-through."

Looking down, all she saw was dirty streaks on her white skirt and pink blouse and the perfect outline of her lacy bra. Groaning, she leaned against the table to wait until everyone was gone. She wasn't fit for public anymore.

But the minute everyone was gone, she could hightail it home and get out of the hot church. And away from the hot preacher.

CHAPTER 7

RUSTON WAS happy to finally see the last of the invited guests depart the church. Patrick had invited everyone to the reception since the food had already been paid for. Then people would have the chance to talk to others about what had happened. Then, by the time Natalie resurfaced, most of the gossip would be over.

Walking to the back of the now silent but still hot church, he opened the door to the room he had left Hazel in around half an hour ago. There she sat on the table in the room, playing on her phone. John Henry was on her lap, but he was sound asleep. He had half expected her to be gone, to have snuck out while he was busy. Again. But here she was, still looking a little worse for wear from climbing out the window into the rain. Mia had told the story to him, and he was amazed Mia had gotten the young woman out the window. Both of them, actually.

Giving her a smile, he whispered so as not to wake the boy, "Everyone's gone except the wedding party. They're changing still."

"Good." She did not whisper.

Sitting up, she started to shift the little boy so she could carry him. But Ruston grabbed the little guy from her lap before she could get him and lifted him into his arms, resting him on his shoulder and offering his hand to help her off the table.

He could tell she hesitated a little before she placed her hand in his and let him pull her off the table and onto the floor. Watching her sliding back into her sandals she had kicked off at some point, he didn't let go of her hand.

Nor did he let go of her hand to open the door to the sanctuary. She had to do it. Walking though the sacred hall, he couldn't help but wonder if this was his future. Hazel and the boy in his arms. It felt right as they walked.

As they walked, they could hear people talking in the basement, and he felt Hazel hesitate. So, at the top of the stairs, he sat on the top step and was happy when she did too. They could hear people talking but not what they were saying.

"Do you know any of the bridesmaids?" They had gone to school together, and it was a small town. Hazel probably knew all of them.

"No, they're her college friends and some of his relatives," she answered.

"Did you and Natalie go to college together?" He turned so he could rest his back against the wall and leaned a little so the boy might be more comfortable.

"No, she went to Fargo, and I went to Grand Forks. But we didn't really go at the same time anyway. I went right after graduating, and she skipped a year due to her injuries." She turned slightly toward him.

"Did you finish?"

"No, I made it two years and then came home. It was too hard with John Henry and no help down there. I could farm with Grandpa while Grandma watched him. It's worked out."

"What did you go for?"

"Agribusiness, but I never got past generals." She looked at her son in his arms.

"Do you like farming?" He was watching her eyes. They showed more pain now than when she had fallen into the room from the rain.

"It's okay. I understand it, and it comes easy."

"But you don't love it." He knew she didn't by her previous answer.

"Not love, I guess."

"Why did you go for that then?"

"Grandpa wants to hand the farm down to one of his grandkids. That's me. I'll keep it going for John Henry." She looked at her hands.

"So, you plan to farm until this guy is an adult and hope that he wants to farm?" he asked.

Since he had met the family, he had been calling the boy just John, like his grandfather. But he now knew the boy was also named after her brother. John Henry was what everyone but her grandparents called him.

"Sounds dumb now, but it's the plan." She shrugged.

"How about Hazel? What does she want to do?" He ran his hand up and down the boy's back.

"Hazel doesn't get a say anymore. She will do what is expected of her now. Everyone is counting on her."

He let her get off with the answer that wasn't an answer at all.

"How old is he?" Ruston pointed at the boy on his back.

"Three, he'll be four at Christmas time. He is what I do. I do every-thing for him." She leaned forward to touch the boy on his back, running her hand over where Ruston's hand had just rubbed.

"What's the story of him?" he asked, wondering if she would answer. It was a very personal question, he realized only after he had asked.

"Too much booze, too much fun, and boom—a baby on the way. The dad didn't want to believe he was his, so I let it go. I had enough love for him for two." She scooted closer and brushed the hair out of the boy's face.

"That's it, no great love story?" He looked into her hazel eyes.

"Nope."

"I didn't realize until after you left that we had used protection." He realized it was the first time in his life he wished he hadn't. Having a child with Hazel didn't scare him at all. Not like it should.

Her only response was a shrug as her eyes snapped from her son to his.

"It's just most of the time it is foremost on my mind. That night was the first time it got away from me." He held her eyes as he said it.

"Yeah, it was intense. Sorry." She turned away from him, her eyes on the floor again.

Her apology made him laugh out loud, then suppress it as the boy moved in his arms at the sudden sound. "You're apologizing for the best sex of my life."

At his words, she blushed. She was actually blushing for him. If he didn't already have a little boy in his arms, he would have pulled her into them.

"Can we not talk about that here?" She raised her arms to the church ceiling.

"Okay. How often do you crash parties to sing?" he asked and was rewarded by another blush.

"I don't crash parties. I am always invited. I follow the band around, and they let me play when they are on break. Just a few songs. I get to go about once a month. I can't leave John Henry with Grandma all the time. I might have to quit going if I keep going to book club. It's getting too much for my grandparents to watch him all the time." She just looked at the little guy in his arms.

"You're always saying that, that you feel you're relying on them too much for help. I bet they love watching him." His own parents loved every moment they were with their grandkids.

"Oh, they love him. But he gets busy, and they sometime lose him in the house. He likes to hide from them."

"Maybe you could just bring him to book club."

"No, I'm the only one who has kids. I don't want to be that person who always brings her kids to stuff. And we talk about killers, not appropriate."

"I have your shoes," he said.

She looked down at the sandals she was wearing and wiggled her toes. "I think they're comfortable. Do you like them?"

Again, he let out a loud laugh and had to resettle the boy on his chest. "No, I don't have your shoes. I have the boots you left at the party."

"Oh, it seemed odd that you would have women's sandals, but I didn't want to judge." She flashed him a dimple, and his heart almost melted on the spot.

"They're in my office."

"Did you grab my underwear?" she asked so innocently.

"No, did you leave them also?" He wanted to laugh at her expression and regretted that he hadn't noticed them that night. Because he would have grabbed them also. But he might not be as quick to return them.

"I did, and I liked that pair, too."

"Do you like your hair like this better or all spiky?" He ran his hand over John Henry's.

"It more fun when it's spiky, as you call it. Makes me seem more fun. Flat is easier to do on a day-to-day basis." She touched her hair as she said it.

"Would you ever make it spiky and sing to me again? It's a real turn-on," he whispered the last sentence.

"No, preacher man, you are not to be turned on." She tipped her head back as she laughed at her joke. "Did you think that Natalie would bolt?" she asked when she stopped laughing.

"I had my suspicions that she wasn't as happy as she had thought she would be," he admitted.

"Yes, she was in love with the idea of getting married and then being able to leave here. But really, she loves it here. She always has," Hazel said.

"She spent a lot of time at the rehearsal dinner wanting to be with the book club and not her closest friends."

"I can see that. We're fun." She flashed the dimple his way.

"Why weren't you there last night?" He wanted to know. Not just because Natalie had talked to him. He had wondered even before that.

"I had to choose between the wedding and the rehearsal dinner. Grandma didn't want to watch him for both. In the end, she didn't want to watch him today either, so he came with me. Sometimes I have to be a mom, even when I don't want to be." Her smile contained no dimple, no joy.

"I want to take you out on a date sometime. I want to get to know you better, Hazel May." At that point, her son lifted his head from his chest, looked him right in the eyes, and panicked.

Hazel pulled him onto her lap and soothed the boy, making his world right again. Seeing her with her son made him think her true calling was being a mother, having a dozen of these little things. Maybe they would all look like her, just like John Henry.

When she got him calm, she stood up. "I have to go."

"Are you going to the reception?" he asked, standing also.

"No, I should get him home." She headed down the stairs away from him.

"Maybe just for a little bit?" he pressed, following her.

"No, I should be getting home," she insisted as she opened the door to the wet landscape. It had stopped raining, but the air and ground were still wet.

"How about the date?" he asked again, seeing if she would answer this time.

"No, Ruston, we are not compatible. I can tell you that without wasting your time," she said without looking at him. Just looking at the wet outdoors.

"We seem pretty compatible, Hazel. We get along and have fun together, I think."

"Yes, we do, but there's still a big difference that would always hang over us until it crushes us." She looked up at the sky as she said it.

"What is that? I can't think of what could be so hard to overcome." He touched her shoulder.

Turning, she looked him right in the eyes, something she rarely did. Her hazel eyes bore into his. "I don't believe in your God, Ruston. He abandoned me a long time ago, and I cannot forgive him for that."

Turning, she walked out the door into the rain with her son in her arms. Ruston was stunned that she would say it out loud. He had suspected as much, but to actually hear her say the words? He didn't follow as he watched her go. Her reasoning was correct; it was the only thing that would crush any relationship they would ever have.

CHAPTER 8

IN THE TWO months since Natalie's failed wedding, Ruston had seen Hazel nine times: each Sunday when she sat in the pew with her grandparents. Each Sunday, she had sat with them, stood with them, but had not participated in any ritual that involved more than being in attendance. Ruston had watched her every Sunday for a sign that maybe she was ready for something. Every Sunday, he greeted her after the service, but she still did not shake his hand. Sometimes she couldn't even meet his eyes.

Each Sunday, he watched the family as he led the service. He noticed that the older couple were looking more tired than others in his congregation, or maybe it was just him projecting onto the couple, who were pulling back from helping Hazel when she needed them. He had noticed that even though John Henry was now sitting in the pew next to his mother, he sat on the other side of her, away from the older couple.

He hadn't seen the family in town at all. No run-ins with Hazel. Had she gone to sing at a party in the last two months? He had almost tried to find out who the band was that was playing that night, but he had no idea where to start. And he knew he wouldn't be going to a party again.

Natalie hadn't come back to talk to him about Hazel after her honeymoon. Well, not a honeymoon, the couple didn't go anywhere, but she had left for a week and had come back in high spirits and had almost immediately started to date a teacher friend of her father's. They seemed happier than she had been with her fiancé. He hoped the two young women had been able to work things out together without his help. Either way, Natalie hadn't spoken to him about Hazel once since coming back.

He was sitting in his office writing his sermon for Sunday. It was Friday, so he didn't have a lot of time to get it done. It was almost five when he heard someone come into the church. When it was quiet, he could hear when the outside door opened.

Hazel? His heart flipped at the thought that she would come.

Jumping out of his chair, he looked up at the shelf that still held her boots. He still had not given them back to her. Seeing them still on the shelf was weird and comforting at the same time.

Walking out of his office, he almost ran into Natalie Beckett. Her face was stricken. Grabbing the young woman, he asked, "What's wrong, Natalie?"

"Hazel," was all she said, a little out of breath.

"What about Hazel?" he demanded a little too harshly, but he was starting to panic.

"Her grandpa had a heart attack. He's in the hospital. But she's home with just John Henry." She pulled out of his arms but grabbed his hand and started to pull him along with her. "She won't go to the hospital. She needs all of us there."

Whoever "all of us" are, Ruston didn't care. Without a word, he followed the tall young woman out of the church. Stopping, he locked the door and ran to the curb, where her SUV was sitting, still running. They didn't speak as she drove them out of town.

As they sped toward where Hazel was, he realized he had no idea where she even lived. No idea at all. On a farm was all he knew. Driving past farm after farm, he forced himself to try and calm the woman driving the car. "What happened?"

"He and Hazel were out working in the field, harvesting. He just fell over. She called 911, and an ambulance took him away. That was a few hours ago. Her grandma called Mia at the café not that long ago, and we're all heading out there. She's been alone all this time." Natalie was trying not to panic.

Ruston was doing the same thing.

What she didn't say was that she might only be one panic attack away from not being able to breathe on her own. That she gets suicidal sometimes before she has a panic attack and after. But he noticed Natalie was going close to ninety on the loose gravel road.

"Has she improved since your wedding?" he asked.

"Yes, she seemed too. We talked after I got back. I forced her to talk to me since we needed things out in the open. It's helped, but this could be too much," Natalie said as she slowed.

"I'm worried too," he admitted as she turned into a yard that had a large square house and a large red barn. Searching the yard, he didn't see Hazel or John Henry.

They both jumped out of the car and heard John Henry crying in the house. Looking around the yard and the field beyond, he saw her in the middle of the field, just sitting in the dirt.

"She's in the field. You go get the baby, I will go to her." He ran off, not letting Natalie argue with him.

Slowing when he got close to her, she faced away from him, looking straight ahead. Did she even notice he was there? When he got close to her, she asked, "Is he dead, too?"

"No, he's stabilized." He sat down next to her and pulled her into his arms and onto his lap. She was thinner than she had been two months before, light and more fragile.

"But he's going to," she whispered.

"One day, we all do. But not today." He rocked her like a little child.

Silently, they sat rocking in the middle of the wheat stubble. Neither talked or cried. She hadn't cried yet, he could tell. Maybe the pain was beyond tears. Another sudden death amongst too many in her life.

"I'm sorry they made you come out. You have more important

stuff to do. You know, talk to God and all." She pushed herself out of his arms.

"Nothing is more important than you, Hazel." He pulled her back into his arms.

"They shouldn't have called you." She pushed her way out of his arms completely.

"I'm glad they did." He got up and pulled her to her feet.

"You probably shouldn't be. I told them." Hazel walked toward the house.

"Told them what?" he asked from behind her, watching her jean-clad butt as she walked.

Turning, she caught him looking and smiled with the dimple. "I told them you said all kinds of curse words when you were fucking me."

Taking a quick step forward, he put his arms around her and kissed the smiling face with the dimple. No light kisses this time; it had been far too long since their last kiss. A kiss like she gave him the night of the party. He didn't even care who saw him. He had wanted to do this since she left him in bed that night. Sliding his hands into her short blonde hair, he groaned as her nails scraped his skin through the shirt on his back. Gently, he held her head so she couldn't pull away.

She continued to kiss him back with equal fervor.

"Damn it," he said as he pulled his mouth from hers. Resting their foreheads together, he realized that she was breathing just as heavy as he was. Looking into her hazel eyes blazing with desire, he whispered, "Fuck, hell, damn woman."

"Feeling's mutual, preacher man." She smiled with full dimple at him.

Letting go of her hair and head, he grabbed her hand and walked back toward the house. As they made it into the yard, he noticed more cars were there. The book club, he assumed.

When they came around the house, he saw the book club were all there, sitting at a picnic table with their significant others. All were in couples except Mia, Mandy, and Hazel. But maybe he could do something about Hazel soon. Maybe he had given up too soon on a relationship with her.

John Henry ran to them when he saw his mom. His tears seemed to have been calmed with a sucker. As the boy got close, Ruston reached down and picked up the little guy, who settled happily in his arms.

"How are you, Haze?" Mia gave her a hug, but Hazel didn't let go of his hand.

"Okay for now. I don't know about later," she admitted.

"At least Ruston was here to help out," Ruth said, but Anderson poked her in the side for saying it.

"True." Tess nodded in agreement. "I don't think any of us would have given you that kiss."

At her words, everyone broke out laughing, except the couple who had exchanged the kiss—they both blushed and looked at each other.

"Come on, let's see if there's anything too eat. It's food time." Mia led them all into the house.

Ruston had to let go of her hand because John Henry was wiggling too much. Once he did, she wandered into the house with Natalie. He watched the taller, darker woman give her a hug as they walked. They seemed to be getting along better than at the time of the wedding.

CHAPTER 9

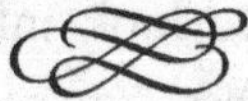

HANGING UP THE PHONE, Hazel placed it on the bed in front of her. Her grandfather was stable but not doing as well as the doctors had thought that he would be doing by now. Her grandmother was staying in town with him.

She glanced over at her son, who was sound asleep in the crib next to her. He had crashed while Tess had held him—Tess had said she could put babies to sleep, but Hazel hadn't believed her at the time.

The group had spent very little time together with their significant others, but it seemed they were getting along just fine. And all had taken to the little boy, and then Math's three kids joined the group as the day got later. Maybe they wouldn't mind if she had to take him to book club on Sunday. She could tell them she wouldn't have a sitter. Just once to see how it worked out.

Getting up, she went down the stairs and saw that the crowd had thinned while she was on the phone. The only ones left were Tess and Math with his kids and Ruston. They were sitting in the living room talking about religion, of course.

The couple was sitting on the couch across from Ruston. Hazel was happy to see they were holding hands. They were so cute together, the big-time bank president and the farmer. Opposites from the outside but devoted to each other even after such a short time.

"What do you think?" Math was asking Ruston.

"I think Math has to realize that Tess has to decide that for herself. It is her choice to become part of the church, not yours," he told Math.

"But she attends, so why not just become a member?" Math argued, more with Tess than with Ruston.

"Math, I think you have to look into your heart and see if you would change religions for Tess. You're asking her to change something very important to her because of you. Is it possible that she would be considering it more if you were more committed to each other?" Ruston asked him, and Hazel looked at Tess, who was pretending to be very interested in the pattern on the couch.

"I have asked her to marry me. She said no," Math stated at Tess.

"I said, Mathias, that it's too soon," Tess defended herself.

"Marriage or not, Math, Tess is there beside you every week. Pledging herself to your faith is a big step, one she might not be ready for." Ruston touched Hazel's leg as he spoke, whether because she was there or because he was telling her that also, she didn't know. Though they were far from getting married, and she was never going to accept God again. No God would do what his had done to her.

Their relationship, or lack of it, came down to her not believing in the one thing that was most important in his life. He dedicated his life to serving something she had no interest in.

Curling her feet under her, Hazel realized she had become the topic of conversation. Her eyes opened. Had she fallen asleep? All three were looking at her.

"What?" she asked.

"I just wanted to know if you want me to come by tomorrow and finish off the wheat harvest?" Math had asked.

She sat up. "Why?"

"Because you need to get it off, I am done with wheat now, and it will take about a day. Maybe we can get Tess to run the combine." He squeezed his girlfriend's leg.

"No, I couldn't let you do that. I can get it done." Even as she said it, she didn't know how she would have time with no one to watch John Henry.

"No, Hazel, we will be here in the morning. No is not an answer. I will call the book club. It's Saturday, so everyone should be off but maybe Mia. We'll get it done." Tess got up and hugged Hazel, who had tears in her eyes. She really hadn't thought about how she was going to finish everything with her grandfather in the hospital. Doing it alone would take weeks.

"Okay," she whispered into the hug.

"We'll be back in the morning," Math said as he pulled his girl-friend out of the house.

"See you in the morning," Tess said as she went.

"Bye." Hazel followed them to the door and watched them go to their car.

As their car drove out of the yard, Ruston came up behind her and put his arms around her. "Now I'm stuck."

"What?" she asked, loving the feeling of his arms around her.

"Natalie drove me out, but she left without me," he replied into the back of her head.

"Oh, I guess you can take my car. I can use the pickup if I need to go anywhere. Or if you come back tomorrow, you can catch a ride back to town then," she said, but she leaned back into his chest.

"Do you want me to go, Hazel?" he whispered in her ear.

"No, but you can't stay." She wanted to be in his arms, but she knew he had an image to maintain. Staying here would jeopardize his job.

"I have no car out front. Only your friends know that I am even here, and you said most of them know we have already slept together."

"Yeah," she said breathlessly as his hands slid up over her breasts, with only a shirt and bra between them.

"Can I stay, Hazel?" he asked again.

"Please stay, Ruston," she said as his lips touched her neck. But at her words, he spun her around and pinned her against the wall with her hands over her head as he continued the kiss they had started in the field a few hours before.

With her hands pinned over her head by one of his, she was unable to touch him like she wanted to. She was unable to pull her arms free. His free hand had slipped up under her shirt and bra and was caressing her breast, making her want to watch him more.

Pulling her mouth from his, she trailed kisses across his face, and as his lips went back to her neck, she licked his ear and hissed, "Let me go, preacher man."

"No, you go too fast. I want to take my time." He was breathless as he said the words.

"Fuck." She threw her head back to give him better access to her neck as she wrapped a leg around his waist to pull him closer. When she got the other around him, he pinned her against the wall with his body and finally let go of her arms.

With her hands suddenly free, she pulled his shirt from where it was tucked into his pants, then started fumbling with the shirt's buttons. But it just kept her busy while he pulled her away from the wall and held her in place while he started walking. As she worked the buttons, he made it to the top of the stairs and asked, "Which is yours?"

Stopping, she looked at him and said, "John Henry is in mine."

"Where then?" he said as they just oddly stood in the hallway. She had never brought a man home, never even thought about it.

Looking around, she wondered what to do. The other two rooms were still her siblings' rooms. Nothing had changed in them since the day they died. The other room was just full of junk; there wasn't even a bed or anything. Her grandparents had a room downstairs. She pushed away from him, and he lowered her to the floor. Talk about breaking the mood.

"There is no place. I'm sorry. You can take my car home." She turned and walked away from him. Pushing the door open to her bedroom, she crawled into the twin bed she had always slept in. After a few minutes, she climbed out long enough to strip out of her clothes and climbed back into the bed.

Rolling over, she watched her son sleeping in the crib next to her.

Don't cry, Hazel, she demanded. *You know it was better not to have him again. There's no future in it.*

She saw the hallway light turn off before her bedroom door opened. Ruston walked into the room and looked around in the dark. What did he see? A crib and dresser and a twin bed. Nothing.

"Can I stay?" he asked.

"Yes," she answered, then watched as he took off his clothes. First his shirt that only had a few bottom buttons left. Then his T-shirt and slacks. Sitting on the bed, he took off his socks. She scooted close to the edge of the bed. He would have to lie close to the wall in case John Henry woke up.

Awkwardly, he climbed in over her, and when he was settled, he pulled her into his arms. Ruston just held her and let his body warm her, taking away the cold that had seeped into her.

"What's in the other rooms?" he whispered, not wanting to wake the baby in the crib right next to the bed they were in.

"One is storage, one is Henry's, and one is Hanna's. We don't go into them. This has always been mine," she whispered back.

Under the covers, he pulled her closer to his warm body. "So, your whole life is this little room, and John Henry sleeps in it too?"

"Yes. I should move him into another room, but I don't have it in me. Who will lose their room for my son?" she asked the darkness.

"Nobody. They don't need a room anymore, Hazel. But you and John Henry do," Ruston whispered.

"But they hated when I went into their rooms. I didn't belong there," she said as the tears started to run down her face and into her pillow.

"Don't cry, Hazel." He lifted his head and kissed her bare shoulder.

"I don't want to. Make it stop, Ruston. Please. Take the pain away." She rolled to face him and ran her hands up his bare chest. Once they made it all the way up, she let them go, wrapping her arms around his head so that she could pull his lips to hers. The kiss was not the deep, hungry kiss of earlier, but soft and tender.

He carefully pushed her onto her back as the kiss deepened. His hands went to her bare breasts under the covers, and she sighed as he caressed them, making her nipples pebble under his touch. Pulling his mouth from her, he kissed down her face and neck. Lightly he brushed his teeth over her skin, reminding her of the hickey she had given him the first time. She giggled and covered her mouth with her hand and looked over at her son. He was still sleeping. Turning back to Ruston, he was looking at her. Smiling, he took her nipple into his mouth and sucked gently, leaving the hand on her mouth as she moaned as quietly as she could.

As his mouth captured her other breast, his hand slid down her stomach and slipped between her legs. Spreading her legs to give him better access, his fingers worked their magic, and soon her hand wasn't able to contain the sounds she was making.

As she lost control of her ability to stay quiet, his mouth covered hers, and she moaned as she came. Their kiss deepened as he slid between her legs. She could feel his erection press against her, and she shifted her hips in hopes of getting him to slide in.

"Do you have protection?" he whispered as he nibbled on her ear.

"I'm on the pill." She sighed and wrapped her legs around him as he entered her.

Slowly and silently, he pulled in and out as her hips matched his easy rhythm. Letting him take control, she just enjoyed the feeling of him touching her, caressing her, being inside her. Her eye caught his, and she smiled at him, then bit her bottom lip to stop the moan from leaving her mouth. His eyes flared with desire, and his tempo increased, making it harder to control the noises coming from her.

His mouth clamped over hers as she came, losing her ability to be quiet, and she moaned into his mouth, matching his groan as they came together.

Laying with him on top of her, both breathing heavily, she glanced over at her still-sleeping son. Then she turned back to Ruston and kissed him, running her hands through his curly hair. Since their activities had made him sweat, his hair was slightly damp, making the curls more pronounced. Adorable.

He rolled them onto their sides, looking at each other. He ran a thumb over her cheek and down to her chin. Then he lightly pressed a kiss to her lips, then her cheek.

"I didn't think you would be quiet enough. I thought you would wake him for sure," he whispered.

"Me too." She couldn't believe the boy was still sleeping.

"Goodnight, Hazel May." He kissed her nose.

"Goodnight, Pastor Ruston." She turned in his arms so that her back was pressed to him.

He pulled her close and kissed her shoulder, then her head.

Hazel felt Ruston's breathing even out as she lay beside him, watching her son sleep. She had no idea what the future held for her or Ruston, but she would enjoy the present for as long as she could.

Her eyes drifted close as she thought about the next day with Mathias Nordskov's help with the harvest. It was going to be way different than what she and her grandfather did. Would she enjoy it? She would find out tomorrow.

CHAPTER 10

RUSTON HAD WOKEN in the middle of the night with Hazel in his arms, so he pulled her closer to him as he lay in the dark little room and listened to her breathe. There was not a lot of room in the little bed they shared, but in his mind, it was perfect. She was perfect.

Running his hand lightly down her body, he smiled into the darkness when she moaned in her sleep. Though the two times they had sex were completely different, Ruston couldn't decide which one was better. He was sure that as long as it was with Hazel, he was happy just to be with her.

Kissing the top of her head, he drifted off to sleep again, content with her in his arms, warm and soft pressed against his body.

The next time he opened his eyes, the body pressed against his was a lot smaller and rounder. John Henry was sound asleep in the spot Hazel had been. Looking around the room, he didn't see her anywhere. Shifting a little to sit up, the boy's eyes popped open and looked at him.

Oddly, he realized he had never been alone with the little boy. Hazel rarely let the boy out of her arms. Hazel's eyes looked back at him from her son as the boy sat up. Wearing little blue pajamas, he analyzed the man who was in his mother's bed. Ruston was confident the boy had never seen a man in his mother's bed before.

Ruston was sure the boy was about to cry, but then he smiled a big smile that brought out two dimples in his cheeks. One more than his mother had.

The little boy leaned over to Ruston and ran a hand over his hair. "Bless you," the boy said in recognition of who Ruston was.

With a smile, Ruston copied the boy, making John Henry giggle. Then he said, "I am Ruston. Can you say Ruston?"

The little boy frowned at Ruston. Did he understand? Ruston had actually spent very little time around little kids. Sure, his brothers had kids, but he didn't spend time one on one with any of them. Was he even any good with kids?

Before he could figure out what to talk to a little boy about, he was trapped in bed since he was not wearing any clothes. John Henry climbed off the bed but soon came back with a book. Handing it to Ruston, he plopped himself down right next to him. Shifting himself up so he could lean against the headboard, he pulled the boy next to him and started to read.

After he had read it once, John Henry was still looking at the book and said, "Again." So, Ruston started it again, this time pointing out the animals on the pages and adding voice changes to the characters.

Glancing up, he saw Hazel standing in the doorway. She was fully dressed for the day and was just watching him, holding a coffee cup in her hand. Smiling at her from next to her son, he tapped the bed for her to sit. Still holding the coffee cup, she walked into the room and sat next to him, nearly touching because the bed was so small.

"Morning, Hazel." He rested a hand on her leg, needing the little bit of connection.

John Henry instantly crawled onto her lap and snuggled in tight. "Mommy."

"Morning, boys." She handed Ruston the cup, trying not to spill it as her son wiggled onto her lap.

"Mommy." John Henry sat up and put his hands over Hazel's cheeks so that she was looking at him. "That is Ruston."

"I know, baby boy. His name is Ruston." Hazel smiled with her dimple when she said the words. "Let's go make breakfast, so he can get up." She gave him a wink as she got up and gathered the boy into her arms.

Ruston watched her climb off the bed with the little boy in her arms, watching her hips sway as she left the room, humming a song as she went. *At least she has no regrets*, Ruston thought as he climbed out of the bed. Grabbing his clothes, he went to the bathroom to get ready for the day. He would have to run home before people started showing up. No way was the book club going to see that he was wearing the same clothes as yesterday.

Frowning, he wondered if that felt like he was ashamed of what had happened last night. He knew he wasn't—he wanted to tell everyone he was in love with her, that he wanted to spend the rest of his life waking up to her. Or even to her kids. But he also knew that Hazel wasn't ready to declare anything to him or the world. There were issues she had to work out before there could be a future for them. He hoped those issues could get resolved sooner rather than later.

Once dressed, he left the bathroom, and he could hear her singing downstairs. She sang when she was happy. He was proud it was him that had made her happy. He was happy too.

Knowing she was downstairs and occupied for a minute, he walked over to a closed door and opened it. This was a big intrusion on Hazel's family, but he needed to see. The door opened to another small room, like Hazel's. This one also had a twin bed, a dresser, and a nightstand. It felt much roomier, but it was missing the crib and toys that hers had. The bedspread was blue, and the car posters on the wall told Ruston that this was Henry's room. A few posters had fallen on the floor, and the bedspread was crooked on the bed. There was a good amount of dust on everything, and a small population of dead flies lay on every surface. Other than the dust and bugs, it looked like the kid was coming off the bus at any moment. The room was completely trapped in time, never moving forward.

Shutting that door, he opened the next one, but it was much the same as the other. Bed, dresser, nightstand, dust, dead flies, and posters falling off the walls. But this room was a little more cluttered. Papers were on the desk, and books were scattered in different areas of the room. On the bed was a book, open and dusty.

Closing the door, he could believe that the rooms had actually been left untouched by everyone in the house for almost six years now. Hazel had brought home a new life to raise in this house, and she had to keep him in her room with her. Who wouldn't clean out one of those rooms for that little boy? Those kids were never going to be here again, but Hazel and John Henry were here every day.

Hazel would never get over that day if it greeted her every time she passed these rooms. The living triplet needed closure that this situation would not let happen. And she needed closure to stop the pain she was constantly in.

Happily, she was still singing in the kitchen when he made his way into the room. The radio was playing, and she was singing along. John Henry was sitting on the counter eating a waffle and wiggling along with his mom's dancing. Walking up behind her, he slipped his arms around her and pulled her back to him. Her movements stopped, and she leaned back into his body.

"Don't stop singing, Hazel," he said into her neck as his lips grazed her soft skin. "I love it when you sing."

"I'm no good at it," she argued as she pulled away and took John Henry off the counter, placing him on the floor.

When he pulled her back to him again, they were face to face. "Dance with me then."

She did. Throwing her arms around his neck, she tapped the beat against the back of his neck. Quietly, she leaned her head onto his chest as they danced slowly through the kitchen. One song ended and another began, but still they danced. And she hummed along.

"You still have no rhythm," she murmured into his chest.

"You will have to teach me," he responded, wanting to dance with her every day.

Ruston felt a tug at his leg, and he lifted John Henry into his arms, and they continued to dance. After a song or two, the boy got tired of it and pushed away from them, forcing them apart in the process. Ruston wanted to pull Hazel back into his arms, but John Henry was demanding something to drink.

"Can I borrow your car and go get changed and shave?" he asked.

"Do you have to shave?" she asked, running a hand down his cheek.

"If you let me use your car, I will not shave today. See what you think of the stubble tonight." He winked, hoping to be with her again that night.

Smiling at him, she leaned against the counter. "Keys are in it."

Taking her hand in his, he said, "If I kiss you goodbye, I'll never leave."

He nearly ran to the car in hopes of getting back to her sooner. Climbing into her car, her smell surrounded him. He had no idea where he was. Natalie had driven him out yesterday, and he wasn't paying attention like he should have. Pulling out his phone, he opened the map to get directions, but before he did, he made a location for Hazel's house. When asked what he wanted to name the location, he started typing Hazel's name but instead stopped. On second thought, he typed home. Because suddenly, wherever Hazel was, that was home.

CHAPTER 11

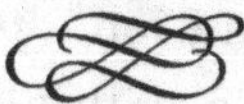

ONCE RUSTON HAD LEFT, Hazel called her grandmother and found out that her grandfather's condition had not changed overnight. Hazel had filled the older woman in on what Math was helping her do that day. Grandma had told her that she should be getting the work done herself, not having her friends do it for her. Hazel knew she was right; she should be doing it herself. If she was going to do this, she had to actually do it. Alone.

After she hung up with Grandma, she went outside and had John Henry run around the yard. With all the courage she could muster, she called Tess and told her that Math need not come over. Hazel would do it herself since it was her job. Not listening to her friend's protest, Hazel hung up.

If this was really what she wanted, she shouldn't need any help. It would take a lot of time, and she had no one to watch John Henry, so he would have to go along with her. Life was hard, but she should be used to that by now. And it wasn't getting any easier anytime soon.

Better start the day. It was going to be a long one.

Walking into the yard, she picked up John Henry as a cloud of dust appeared on the county road. The cloud turned into a small SUV as it turned onto her driveway.

But instead of listening, Tess drove her little red SUV into her yard and stopped by the house. Hazel was in jean shorts and an old T-shirt, but Tess was dressed in black dress shorts and a form-fitting sleeveless blouse that showed off her baby bump. Tess was always dressed ten times better than anyone else.

"This is me saying no to your 'I do not need your help' Hazel," Tess said.

"I shouldn't need help. It's my job."

"What are you going to do with him?" Tess asked, pulling John Henry from her arms.

He went to her willingly.

"I can keep him with me. It'll be fine," she argued, though she had never been successful in that. John Henry hated just sitting around, and hours on her lap in a tractor or combine would be just that.

"It is not fine. What happened? Last night you were all for this. Now you do not need anyone?" Tess demanded, her eyes on the field that needed to be harvested.

"Nothing. I just grew up. I should do it myself." Hazel looked out at the field, realizing just how daunting it was, how much time it was going to take.

"Should. You keep saying should. Yes, you could do it yourself. And I have no doubt that you would do it yourself. But you keep saying should. Who told you that you do not need help?" Tess shifted the boy in her arms as she looked at Hazel in question.

"Nobody," Hazel replied as she watched a red combine slowly drive toward them. She should have known it would take more than a phone call to stop the book club.

"Ruston? Would he say that?" Tess asked, looking over Hazel's shoulder at the road, seeing the same thing Hazel was.

"No, he would never do that." Hazel shook her head.

"That is how I read him also."

They watched a car pull into the yard. Natalie was there.

The car was barely stopped when Tess stomped over to her. Natalie looked at them with a smile before Tess jumped in with, "Someone told Hazel she didn't need help with the wheat. Do you know who that would be? She says it's not Ruston. Do you think it's Ruston?"

Natalie instantly lost her smile. "No, not Ruston, but her grandparents wouldn't want anyone's help. I can just hear her grandma say that she needs to learn to do things on her own; nobody will be around to help her."

Hazel wouldn't confirm or deny anything. It didn't matter—she had a job, and she didn't need help.

Tess handed John Henry to Natalie, then turned to Hazel, pulling her into a hug. "She's wrong, Hazel. You take help any chance you get. Nobody does it all without help. We all are coming because we want to help you. Because we all love you, Hazel."

"But you guys have better things to do than help me. I can get it done. Don't worry about it," Hazel said with less conviction as the combines grew closer. There were now two heading her way.

"We have nothing better to do than be there for you. You are more important than anything we could have possibly done today." Tess pulled her into her arms as Hazel tried to control the tears.

It had been years since anyone had said they wanted to help her. Years since anyone had helped her without her having to beg. She was so tired of begging.

"Tess is right, Hazel. We're all here to help you today. But we are also here to help you every day. Any one of us can watch John Henry. Any one of us can come out here and help with stuff. We are friends, and that's what friends do." Natalie put her arm over Hazel's shoulders and kissed her temple. "Tess especially—she needs practice with kids."

"I do not," Tess stated firmly and then broke out laughing. "I know more about kids than both of you put together."

"A few months pregnant, and she thinks she's an expert," Natalie teased Tess and let Hazel go.

Just then, the combines turned onto the driveway. They were twice the size of the one her grandfather had. Math was driving one, and Tess's nephew was in the other. He and his family hadn't been in town long, and Hazel didn't know him well, but Hazel knew he was one of Math's best employees since arriving.

As three trucks followed the combines, then two cars behind them, everyone was there to help her. Hazel knew she couldn't stop them from helping even if she tried.

By the equipment's size, Hazel knew the crops would be off before sundown, maybe before mid-day. It wasn't going to take long, and for that, she was thankful.

Math in the first combine had stopped near her, and Hazel had climbed up on the large combine and rode with him to the field. Together they devised and planned, and for some reason, Math let her drive the machine that cost more than her farm ever would.

It was a different way of farming that Hazel had never known. New equipment vs. the old, broken-down equipment she always used. A completely different way of operating.

After a few hours, she realized that she didn't enjoy the big new equipment any better than the old equipment that she had always used. Neither really made her happy.

CHAPTER 12

THE COMBINES WERE CIRCLING the fields by the time Ruston had made it back to the farm. He parked the little yellow car, got out, and saw Tess holding John Henry. The boy wiggled free and ran to Ruston, and, with a smile, he caught the little boy in a hug. Carrying him over to the women, he realized Hazel was in the field with the guys.

The book club had actually brought food for lunch. Since they had no idea what Hazel had in the house, they thought it would be easier just to bring out some stuff. They sat in the kitchen chatting about this and that as Ruston played with the little boy.

Soon he was joined by Natalie, who sat across from him and started to push around cars on the carpet.

"The house hasn't changed a bit since I was last here. It's like they're here; I just haven't found them. It's eerie," Natalie whispered to him.

"How does that make you feel?" Ruston asked as the boy grabbed a few more toys from a box in the corner to show him.

"Sad. It's been almost six years," she said. "It's also upsetting because Hazel can't move on if she's reminded of this every day."

"That's what I thought this morning, too," Ruston confided.

"This morning?" Natalie questioned with a knowing smirk. After all, she was the one who had left him here.

"Shit," Ruston said under his breath.

"Hey, I'm not judging. Hazel deserves all the happiness in the world. But if you ever hurt her, I will hurt you."

"I hurt when she hurts," he said with a weary smile, knowing that he wanted to take all that hurt away from her. Never let her hurt again.

"Good." Natalie nudged him with her shoulder.

They played for a little while with the boy until he wandered into the kitchen to get a snack. John Henry recognized an easy mark, and it seemed Tess would give him anything he wanted. Tess wasn't going to tell the boy no to anything.

Ruston stood up and asked Natalie, "Can I show you something?"

He hadn't been able to get the two bedrooms out of his mind since he saw them. They were hovering there, and he knew how Hazel felt. It was just there, and he couldn't get away from it.

Natalie got up wearily. "Okay."

Going up the stairs, he indicated for her to follow. It was a place she was far more familiar with then he was, but it was him leading her through the house. At the top of the stairs, he opened the ghost bedroom of Henry first. "They haven't done anything with these rooms since that day." Going across the hall, he opened the other door, history book still open on the bed. "This is what I saw this morning. She doesn't know that I looked in here."

"Oh my God. I can see them both in there. I expect them to walk in the door at any time—except Henry would never have made his bed, and Hanna would have a pile of clothes on the floor. Someone must have cleaned them up at some point," Natalie said, unable to stop the tears.

"I didn't show you to make you cry. I'm sorry." Ruston pulled her into his arms and held her until the tears disappeared. When they were gone, he let her go and showed her Hazel's room. "Then Hazel lives in this little room."

He wondered what she thought about the little bed and the crib crammed into the tiny room. The room was messy, but there was nowhere to put anything. He knew she could touch the crib while lying in bed; he had seen her do it last night. For most of the little boy's life, she had slept close enough to touch him.

"I think I'm going to cry again. Do you think they won't let her move into one of the other rooms? That they're forcing her into this little room with all her stuff? His stuff?" Natalie asked. Backing away from the room, her friend called home. A room that meant Hazel couldn't move beyond the past. It was alive and well just on the other side of her door.

"I don't know. I think she needs out of this house, though. Maybe away from her grandparents altogether," Ruston replied as they descended the stairs, hating to admit that the older couple might be part of the issue.

"Me too. This is why she can't get over the past. It's still the present for her. Like I said, it feels like they're still here," Natalie whispered so the others wouldn't hear.

As they entered the kitchen, he could smell food being prepared. He had expected that Tess, the bank president, wouldn't help much with the food, but she had jumped in with both feet mixing big bowls of who knows what. They were all here for their friend because she needed help, and there was no way they wouldn't help. Ruston loved them all for just being there.

"Ruth, I need an apartment," Natalie announced to the group.

"Moving out on Sam already? Not going back to your dad's?" Ruth asked from the stove, her eyes never leaving the pot she was stirring.

"It's for Hazel. Two bedrooms, cheap rent. Possibly no rent." Natalie pushed for her friend.

"I really don't have much right now. Tess's place is empty, but it's a one-bedroom," Ruth replied, her attention completely on the pot still.

He had recently heard that Ruth owned around a half dozen buildings in downtown Landstad. Not that he knew much about the woman—she didn't go to his church and wasn't someone he had run into in the years he had been in town. Until now.

Tess looked up at them and grinned. "Maybe she would be okay there for a while until something else becomes available. It won't be long. People are constantly moving, you know."

"Not constantly," Ruth mumbled and then turned to Natalie. "Tess's place for now. Is that good enough for you, Natalie?" Ruth asked.

"No rent, she cannot afford what the bank president paid," Natalie reminded her.

"I think the bank president squeaks when she walks, she's so cheap. But I can wave it for a while," Ruth explained and pointed at Tess.

"Will she even move?" Mia entered the conversation for the first time. Her question was valid. Hazel was stubborn.

"We will have to make her," Ruston stated. He wasn't taking no for an answer.

"This place is trapped in the past. She cannot get away from the past if she lives it every day," Natalie informed them. Not telling them about the upstairs, it probably was just as hard for her to see as Hazel.

"She needs to move out anyway. She's almost twenty-four and has a kid. When is her birthday again, Natalie?" Mia asked.

"Two weeks from now, Monday," Natalie informed her.

"I knew it was close. In the early fall," Mia said.

Ruston left the women in the kitchen plotting and planning Hazel's move. He only hoped that she would be willing to move out of the house she had been raised in. He headed out to the field to talk to her because he needed to go see her grandfather in the hospital. After all, he was the man's minister, even if he was having a difficult time with the man's attitude toward his granddaughter.

When he saw her, she was getting out of the cab of one of the big combines. She saw him and walked toward him, smiling as she came. Meeting in the middle of the field, she indicated she was heading toward the house. And to his surprise, she took his hand as they walked.

Looking down at her, he couldn't see her face because she was wearing a blue hat; one of the men must have given it to her because it looked like it was way too big for her. Probably because she had such fair skin, and she would burn easily.

"How are you doing?" he asked her as they walked.

"Good. It's fun with all the guys out there. It would have taken forever for me to do it myself. They'll be done by mid-day," she said with confidence, her eyes sweeping the field of mostly stubble.

"I'm going to town while everyone is here because I have to visit your granddad in the hospital," he told her so that she didn't think he was leaving for something that wasn't as important as her.

"Okay."

"Are you going to visit him?"

"I don't like hospitals," she said matter-of-factly.

"You should still go."

"I don't know if I can. The nightmares will come back."

"Why don't we try tomorrow? Just try. He would like to see you." He wondered how often she had nightmares without even visiting the hospital. She'd never said anything about them, but they hadn't been together all that long. Were they even together now?

"Will you come back tonight?" Her eyes were on her tennis shoes. Slowing, he lifted her chin with a finger as he promised, "I will plan on it."

"Good," she said on a sigh, but to Ruston, it was a step in the right direction. She wasn't pushing him away.

When they got close to the house, she let go of his hand and went inside. He could hear the women greet her and start chatting more loudly.

Ruston went into the house and motioned for Natalie to come out. Laughing, she left the group, and Ruston asked, "Can I get a lift into town?"

"Sure, since I abandoned you here yesterday." She yelled at the others that she would be right back.

Getting into Natalie's car, he was less anguished than the trip here. But she drove just as fast, far faster than was needed or recommended.

"Thanks for showing me the upstairs. I understand a lot more now than before. For me, it was six years ago, and other than the scars, I have few memories about it." Natalie didn't take her eyes off the road, which was a good thing with the speed they were going.

"I thought you should know so that you would understand what she's going through. She needs our help." He tried not to show how tightly he was holding onto the door.

Natalie let out a breath. "We've been trying, but she doesn't let anyone in."

"Can I ask you a question about the accident?" He knew it was a sensitive subject to Natalie. After all, she had been the one in the car that night.

"Yeah, but there are some things I might not know. I was in a coma for months after." Natalie started to slow the car down.

Letting go of the armrest, he asked, "Did Hanna or Henry live very long after?"

Natalie bit her lip and drove for a while before answering, "No, Sam said they died on scene. Instantly."

"That doesn't make sense then. Hazel doesn't want to visit her grandfather because she hates hospitals. I thought it was connected." He wondered what else it could be from, if not the accident.

"It is, I'm sure. A few months ago, I asked how she found out about the accident. You know, who told her and all that. She said that her grandparents woke her up in the middle of the night and took her to the hospital." Natalie stopped talking, then she stopped the car as she started to cry. "Then they made her identify the bodies, Ruston. She was seventeen, and it was bad. Sam told me that it was closed-casket bad. They made her look at them. I never had to see any of that. I got off easy."

"Damn them. No wonder she has nightmares still." He cursed the couple, hating that he had to go and see them soon.

"That's how I feel. They've made it so much worse for her." Natalie's tears were falling.

Pulling her into his arms, he let her cry for her friend, for a woman who has been hurt so much. How could he possibly heal her if the wound was opened every day? At least Natalie was starting to heal from it.

As her tears dried up, she put the car into gear and continued the drive to town. Neither spoke as town appeared, and Natalie pulled up to his house.

As he opened the door, Natalie put a hand on his arm. "She's worth it, Ruston. I want her to be happy, and you make her happy. You make her the Hazel she used to be."

Stopping, he turned to her and asked, "What was she like before? When you were young?"

"Sadly, I can only answer that by talking about all three. They were different. Even though Hanna and Hazel were identical, they were nothing alike. Hanna was into sports and being popular. She was fun to be around and outgoing. Hazel was artsy and quiet. She lived in Hanna's shadow and was never able to shine. Henry was a lot like Hanna, just a little less, but he was the smart one. He had straight As all the time, and he didn't even try. Now I feel like she tries to be less like Hazel and more like Hanna. But Hazel will never be Hanna, no matter how much she tries. Because she is always the artsy, quiet one deep inside." Natalie looked out the windshield, lost in the past.

"I understand," he said, but he didn't. All he could see her as was the woman she was today.

"I don't think you know, but Hazel can sing. But not only sing— Hazel was all about music growing up. She can play any instrument. She loves to sing, and she's really good at it. Music was her life. She was going to be a singer one day, but she quit after the accident. Dad said he hasn't heard her sing since. Sam said they tried to make her sing at the funeral, but she couldn't. She stood in front of the church and couldn't do it. Who could?" Natalie wiped the tears from her eyes.

"I have heard her sing. She's amazing. She sings to John Henry all the time," he told her.

"I want to hear it again. She told me she had to give up her dream because the others' dreams were dead. I would give anything for them to still be here." Natalie looked away from him and out the driver's window, the guilt of being the sole survivor still there.

He knew he had to get out of there, they were just going to upset each other more, so he opened the door and got out. With a wave, she drove off, and he was alone.

Now he had to go visit a parishioner who he was starting to dislike intensely for how he had treated Hazel all these years—how they both had. Instead of helping her get over the accident and what happened, they had made her relive it every day.

After changing into more formal clothing and driving to the hospital, he walked into the wing he knew John May would be in. Seeing Rose in the waiting room, he went over to her. She looked up as he approached, but she didn't smile.

"How is he?" He sat next to her.

"Not good. They don't have a lot of hope."

Maybe there was no hope because she seemed to have already given up on him.

"Did you want to pray?" he asked since it always made him feel better; always made things look better.

"No. God doesn't listen to me." Rose didn't meet his eyes.

"You'd be surprised, Rose." Ruston hated that her granddaughter would have said the same thing.

"Can we just talk?" Rose asked.

"Sure," Ruston agreed. He was here to help her and John any way he could.

"I was just sitting here thinking about my daughter. She would be forty-five this year, but she died many years ago when the kids were in middle school," Rose said, looking at her hands.

"Sorry to hear." He wondered if Hazel knew that. If the kids had ever been told about their mom.

"I remember when she called and said that if we wanted the triplets, we had to come and get them, or she would put them up for adoption. Triplets, can you believe it? Not married, no job, nothing but a drug addiction she didn't want to control. We should have said no. That's what I know now. Why didn't we just say no and let them go?"

He had no answer. Maybe at the time, they thought they could love the kids. But had they? Instead, he said, "Your heart wanted them. They were a part of your daughter, you and John."

She huffed. "I was selfish, and what did it get me? Nothing. They're gone."

He said with more control than he felt, "Hazel is here, and you have John Henry."

Rose shook her head. "It would have been easier if Hazel had just been in that car too."

"Rose, do not talk like that." He didn't want to hear anyone wish Hazel dead. Especially someone who is supposed to love her unconditionally.

"I never understood Hazel. The other two were easy. Hazel has always had her head in the clouds, letting things happen. No real gumption," Rose mused, more to herself than to him.

"She's been trying to please you," he reminded her, because she needed to be told.

"Then she brought home that baby. I can't raise another baby," she said in disbelief, as if Hazel wasn't there every day taking care of her son.

"From what I've seen, she's raising John Henry." He was not being a supportive pastor anymore. He was defending Hazel because someone had to.

"She goes out and leaves him to read books with her friends. I spend all day with him and then she goes out with her friends."

"She isn't doing that often."

"Often enough. Today she's having her friends finish harvesting for her. Her job." The woman didn't even try to disguise the disgust in her voice.

"Everything suddenly being placed on her shoulders was a surprise. She needs help, Rose. It's a lot of work for one person. And John Henry is too young to go with her," he replied because he knew she came so close to doing everything by herself.

"Her grandfather did it every year with no help. She didn't even try," Rose argued.

"You have to take help when it is offered until John is ready to farm again," he said.

Rose looked at the hospital door across from them. "John is not going to come out of this able to work anymore. I plan to sell the farm and move us to the retirement community. We've wanted to for years, but we couldn't because of Hazel. I know Hazel can't manage it anyway."

"What about John Henry? What if he wanted to farm one day, farm the land his family has always farmed? Be the next generation?" It was why Hazel was farming, for her son's future. Didn't his great-grandparents want that same dream for him?

"I'm not going to wait around for a baby to take over the farm. Look what happened when we waited for Henry to take over? He died," she spat out.

"Does Hazel know? It's her job, her life." Her everything. Had they ever planned to leave it to her? Had they wanted her around?

"She doesn't care about the farm. Never has," Rose said. "Doesn't care about anything, not her grandpa, not me. Has she come to see him, us? No."

"I talked to her, and she doesn't like hospitals." He watched her face, no reaction. Did she even realize what she had done to the child by forcing her to see her siblings' dead bodies?

"She never has." She shrugged, as if she wasn't the reason behind that.

Before what? his mind screamed at the woman. *Before you made her look at her dead siblings?* He needed to get away from her. He was getting madder at her with every word she spoke. "I'm going to go in and pray for John." He got up and walked into the room behind Rose.

In the dim room, he walked to the bed and looked down at the man who was hooked up to beeping machines. He looked old and tired, even though he was sleeping.

Picking up his hand, he prayed for the man to recover and to be a better grandfather to his remaining granddaughter. He prayed that he would recover and finally be the grandfather the woman needed him to be.

CHAPTER 13

THE FIELDS WERE BARE, and the people were gone, and Hazel was alone with John Henry. Though the boy was napping, which meant that Hazel was alone. Sitting on the front porch swing, she lazily let the breeze move her. Her legs were pulled up under her, enjoying relaxing after a busy day.

It was around 2:00 p.m., and everything was done. Well, she had to cultivate, but that could wait for a while. In her heart, she knew it was her last harvest. Even if her grandfather recovered, he would never farm again. She was never going to farm by herself. Today had taught her that she didn't have the heart for it like Math did.

But what did she have the heart for? There was nothing but music that interested her, and music wasn't a job. A job was what she needed to take care of her son. To take care of herself.

From her spot on the porch, she watched a cloud of dust moving down the road toward her house, and when the dust cloud turned into her driveway, she hoped it was Ruston coming back. It was that moment she had no idea what he drove. Which meant she was sure it was him until the SUV stopped and Natalie climbed out of it.

Groaning quietly, she didn't want to talk to Natalie. They tended to just fight or cry when they were together. Now here she was, and Hazel's emotions were not ready for her. She just wanted to be alone. She remained silent as Natalie parked the car and walked toward the house. Maybe she would leave.

"Hazel," Natalie said as she got to the top step of the porch.

"Natalie," Hazel said from her spot, unmoving.

"Ruston called me to tell you he has a parishioner who needs him. He doesn't know when he will be done, so I gave him your cell number. He didn't have it." Natalie sat on the other end of the swing, pushing it into motion.

"Thank you," Hazel said, not looking at her. Until that moment, she hadn't realized they didn't know each other's numbers, that they had missed that step in whatever it was they were doing.

"I could have texted you that, but I want to talk to you."

"We don't do well with talking."

"I know. But we should."

Hazel shrugged at her words. Looking over at her former friend, she saw the changes in the woman who sat beside her from the girl she had been. Always taller than the May girls, Natalie was also darker with olive skin and black hair. But what caught Hazel's eye was a scar she showed in the V neck of her shirt. It was not a faint scar; it was very visible. Until today, Hazel had never seen it.

"Do you have a lot of scars?" Hazel asked, but she knew she did. Though she tried not to, she heard about the damage, the surgeries, the recovery that her friend had gone through over the years.

"Yes." Natalie turned toward her and pulled up her shirt.

Hazel gasped at the white and red lines covering her friend's body, from long to short ones. Some looked bad, some looked okay. One ran from where Hazel had seen it above her shirt to mid-stomach.

"They are my reminder of that day. I think of Hanna and Henry every time I see them."

"I have other reminders. I see them every day when I look in the mirror. I see them age when I know they won't," Hazel whispered.

"They wouldn't want you to live like this." She put her shirt down and looked around the yard.

"I have nothing else. No skills, no money, nothing."

"The book club can figure it out. Mia always needs someone for the café, and Ruth has an apartment for you. She's waving rent until you can get a job that pays."

It seemed she had been planning before Hazel had even thought about that.

"I have no one to watch John Henry," was all she said. It was enough.

Natalie just shrugged. "We'll figure it out. Between the five of us, we should be able to figure something out. We are there for you; you have to know that."

"I'll think about it." Hazel wanted to believe it was that easy. But nothing had ever been easy for her.

"Can I ask how it's going with Ruston?" Natalie turned her body toward her.

She didn't look at her. "There's nothing between us."

"Oh really? You're going to go with that answer? I saw the kiss, and I know he stayed the night." Natalie grinned at her.

"It's not going to lead anywhere. We both know that." Hazel bristled at Natalie's glare.

"I don't think Ruston thinks that."

"I have told him."

"He could lose his job if people found out he was staying here."

"He knows the risk."

"I know he does, and he thinks you are worth it, Hazel. If he isn't worth it to you, you have to stop it."

"I like Ruston. I don't like his job."

"Even if he quit his job, he would still believe what he believes. God would still be important to him." Natalie said the words that Hazel knew were true. You can't separate the man from his beliefs, even if you could separate him from his job.

Looking down at her hands, she admitted, "It's a part of him. I know. It's why I've stayed away from him until yesterday."

Natalie turned in her seat and looked at her closely. "How long have you been staying away from him?"

"Since your wedding, mostly. Before that, I could avoid him easily."

"My wedding?" she asked in surprise. It had been months before.

"You don't remember? Oh, yeah, you weren't there." Hazel laughed at her joke.

Natalie glared at her and then started to laugh with her. "I wish I could forget."

"It was the best wedding I have ever been to," Hazel said, still smiling at the memory of sitting and talking to Ruston while he held her sleeping son. The wedding didn't even cross her mind.

"Haze, I want to tell you that I'm sorry I was a bad friend before the accident and after. I should have called you when I woke up. We should have talked years ago. I let you push me away, I shouldn't have."

"I wouldn't have talked to you, even if you'd tried," Hazel admitted.

"I know that, but I should have tried. Our friendship was worth trying for." Natalie put her hand on Hazel's leg.

They sat in silence for a while as they both got lost in thought. Lost in the past they shared and the one they did not. The wind blew gently around them as they sat swinging.

Pushing herself out of the swing, Hazel said, "John Henry is up. I have to go get him." There had been no sound coming from the house, but she needed away from Natalie, away from the past.

Ignoring anything that Natalie was going to say, she rushed into the house and went up the stairs. To her surprise, John Henry was awake and sitting in his crib. Lifting her son from the crib she knew he was too big for, she set him on the floor. When he didn't move from where she set him, she looked toward the door and saw Natalie had followed her through the house.

"Sorry for the mess. I haven't had a lot of time to clean lately." No amount of cleaning could make the room look any better than it did right now. There wasn't enough room for the stuff in it.

"Do you want me to help you clean out another room? If we do it together, it might not be so bad. He needs his own room." Natalie's eyes looked from one side of the room to the other.

"That's okay. We're just fine." Hazel touched the top of her son's head, who was still standing next to her, but he was looking at Natalie in the door.

"No, you're not. He needs a bed, and you need privacy."

"It's fine," Hazel stated firmly.

"He is going to be four, Hazel. You still have him in a crib. And you live in a shoebox with him. You have to clean one of those rooms for him." Natalie had her hands on her hips in the doorway, blocking Hazel's exit, forcing her to think about those rooms and whose they were.

Sitting heavily on the bed behind her, she buried her face in her hands. "I can't. That would mean they're gone, Natalie. Gone forever."

Natalie sat down next to her and pulled her into her arms. "They are already gone forever, Hazel. You have to let them go. You have to live."

"It's hard to be the one that gets to live," she whispered as John Henry hugged her. She hated that her son was so used to her crying.

"I want to help. I want to be there for you when you need someone, but first we need to make room for you to live. I'm going to get the book club together, and we'll do this. You don't have to both be here. We'll make a room for John Henry. You just have to tell us when to come." Natalie moved back so that she was sitting against the wall, her long legs almost hitting the crib. Hazel moved back to sit next to her former friend.

Maybe just friend now.

Both sat in silence because both knew right now Hazel couldn't agree to what Natalie suggested. Maybe in time, but not that day.

"Girl talk," Natalie said because she always hated silence and inactivity. "A preacher, how weird is that?"

Hazel wiped her eyes and watched John Henry pull a toy from his crib and start to play with it. "I try not to think about it. I see him as a guy, not his job."

"I can see that. He's a nice-looking guy," Natalie agreed with a grin.

"How about you living with a teacher? Do you call him Mr. Sullivan?" Hazel asked with a smirk.

"Only when he gets on my nerves. I am very happy with Sam,"

Natalie admitted, though Hazel already knew that. Anyone who saw them together knew that.

"Does he talk about boring history all the time?"

"Almost never, but he reads about it a lot."

"You always had a thing for him. How many hours were spent coming up with awful things to do to him?" Hazel giggled at their younger selves.

"He told me that the worst thing I did to him was have him look at yours and Hanna's boobs. Do you remember that?" Natalie laughed, but Hazel blushed. Even after all these years, it was still embarrassing.

"Do I remember you two pressuring me into showing a teacher my boobs? No, I have no memory of that. Because I blocked it out." Hazel laughed at the memory.

"You were always easy to get to change your mind. All I had to say is Hanna would do it, and you would be on board," Natalie admitted, scooting onto the bed until her back was against the wall.

"Yeah, I always wanted to be outgoing and fun like her." She had always wondered how Hanna had become so outgoing and her not when they were supposed to be identical.

"And I know she would have killed to be able to sing like you. To be able to play instruments. To have such an amazing ability." Natalie reached out and squeezed Hazel's leg.

"No, she didn't care about any of that." She watched John Henry dig around the room for more toys to play with.

Natalie shook her head. "She said she didn't because you outshined her when you were there. Like sports with you. You let her be the star."

"She wasn't a star, you were. You were amazing." If anyone had missed out on using their talent because of the accident, it was Natalie. Her sports dreams died that night, even if she hadn't.

"*Was* is the key word. I *was* good. I have been able to get past it, but it wasn't easy. Ruston said he heard you sing."

"You talk too much to him." She frowned at her friend, wondering when they were constantly talking.

Natalie grinned at her. "He's my preacher; we talk."

"About me?" she asked.

"Sometimes you come up. When did he hear you? In the shower?" Natalie joked.

"He makes me happy, and I sing when I am happy. I sing with John Henry. We dance too," she admitted, though she wasn't happy all that much before Ruston came into her life.

"God, I hated going to dances with you. You always complained about my dancing."

"You have no rhythm, never have. Ruston has no rhythm either." Hazel wanted to teach him some moves, but she was sure he wouldn't catch on. But she still wanted to try.

"So, you have danced with him?"

"Yes, a few times."

"I will get this information out of one of you."

"I don't kiss and tell."

"How about one for one? I tell you one secret, and you tell me one?" Natalie turned to Hazel and crossed her long legs.

Biting her bottom lip, she looked at her tall friend. Slowly she turned and crossed her legs too, so they were looking at each other. "Okay. You go first."

"My mom doesn't know who my dad is, but he's dark." She waved her hands over her body, "My mom is a pale redhead and short. I'm as much like her as I am with my dad. I still look like nobody, it's weird."

"I can see that now that I know you're adopted. I really should have figured that out by the time we were twelve when you were taller than your dad. And I saw the pictures of your parents all the time, and still, I didn't even think about it. Did Hanna know?" She paused, and Natalie shook her head. Hazel, for some reason, liked that she knew something her sister didn't. Even with so many years after she was gone, it made her feel closer to her friend. Taking a breath, she said, "I used to go to Grand Forks and sing at parties when the band took breaks. They let me sing on stage."

"Wow, did you like it? Of course, you did. You did it more than once." Natalie paused and looked at the ceiling for a second, then Hazel. "Okay, when Sam and I left after the wedding thing, my dad all but said he was okay with Sam and me hooking up, or maybe more like he was okay with it if it was more than a hookup."

"Your dad? He must really like Mr. Sullivan," Hazel said in disbelief.

"Call him Sam. It's weird when you call him Mr. Sullivan."

"Sam then." Hazel tested the name. It was going to take getting used to. "I have no idea who John Henry's dad is. I did a lot of sleeping around in college."

"I figured you had dated him for a while. That you had a romantic story of love and loss."

"No, I would pick up guys at parties and usually have sex at the party. I was pretty out of control. Having him made me realize that that was crazy wrong." Hazel looked at the crib next to the bed as John Henry was pulling his blanket from the bed.

"What's his middle name?" Natalie asked.

"What makes you think it is not Henry?" She leaned over and grabbed her son into her arms.

"Because Henry was always going to name his kid John Henry Beckett May. We were dating then." Natalie pulled the boy onto her own lap.

She shrugged. There was no hiding it. "That's his name. Henry has it written on a piece of paper on his dresser still. I saw it as a sign."

"You named him after me?" Natalie hugged him to her and kissed his cheek.

"You were a big part of my life, even if I hated you. I named him what Henry would have named him. At the time, I had no other ideas." In fact, she hadn't planned on naming him anything until the nurse asked her what she wanted to name him. It was only at his birth that he became real to her, precious to her.

"Can I call him Beckett?" Natalie demanded.

"No." She shook her head.

"I am going to name my first baby after you. Hazel May Sullivan. We will call her Hazy. And when I get mad at her, I'll say HAZEL

MAY!" She yelled the last part, making John Henry laugh in her arms.

"You will want to name your baby Hanna. Hanna May Sullivan," Hazel said. Hanna had been Natalie's friend, not her. Nothing that will ever happen between the two will change that fact.

"I want to name my daughter after the strongest woman I know, so Hazy it is. And I know you will name your next one Hanna. And they will be in the same class and be best friends," Natalie said and broke down laughing.

But Hazel turned serious. "I am not having any more."

"Yes, you will. Ruston probably wants a dozen of them." Natalie laughed some more, John Henry joining in, though he had no idea what they were talking about.

"No, I'm done. No matter what is between Ruston and me, there's no future in it. So just drop it." Hazel started to get off the bed, tired of Natalie suddenly.

"Okay." Natalie put her hands on Hazel's knees to stop her. "Ruston is off-limits."

"Thank you." Hazel stopped moving.

"Just one more." Natalie put her hands over John Henry's ears. "Did you have sex in this bed last night?"

Hazel didn't answer the question but knew her face was beet red, screaming the answer. Biting her lip from answering her friend, she couldn't help but smile.

"How? This is a tiny bed. Was John Henry there?" John Henry pushed her hands off his head.

"Quietly, and since we are not both eight feet tall, we made it work," Hazel shot back at her tall friend.

Natalie laughed at the answer because she was nearly six feet tall, and Sam was taller than she was. Whereas Ruston was about the same height as Natalie, and Hazel was quite a bit shorter than them all.

"We need to get you your own room. Being loud is half the fun." Natalie let the little boy go finally.

"If noise is half the fun, Sam needs to work harder." Hazel laughed, and Natalie joined in.

"Oh, Sam is very good at what he does," Natalie replied and then blushed at what she had said.

"You mean droning on about history?" Hazel teased her. "Does talking about the Revolutionary War turn him on?"

Just then, Natalie's cell phone rang, and she looked at the screen, then looked up at Hazel with a grin on her face. "Sam, we were just talking about you."

Hazel heard Sam respond to her, "Nothing but good things?"

"Always good things, but Hazel says that Ruston is better in bed than you. So, we were thinking that we have to switch partners so I can decide if he is actually better than you." Hazel watched her friend keep a straight face as she said the words.

Hazel did not hear Sam respond to the statement. But maybe it was because Natalie slammed the phone to her chest so she could laugh out loud. The happy tears were coming from her eyes.

Controlling the laugh, she pulled the phone back to her ear. "Hazel says that you're crazy to put up with me. She thinks I was mean to you in high school. Was I mean to you?"

"Yes, Natalie," Hazel heard from the phone.

Hazel said so he could hear, "I will send her home if you promise to ground her."

"I will definitely punish her, Hazel." Sam was laughing as Natalie hung up on him.

Natalie rolled off the bed and said, "I have to get home. Punishment time." But she couldn't control her smile.

Hazel got up and picked up John Henry to follow her through the house. In the living room, she turned and hugged John Henry and, of course, called him Beckett. When she was gone, Hazel was surprised that she had fun with their talk. It reminded her of the past, but in a good way. The good times Hazel usually forgot had happened.

John Henry brought her a book to read to him, and as she read it, she wondered if she could let her friends clean out the bedrooms. Could she let someone else remove their things from their rooms? But maybe it was something she could do for her son. Maybe it was time to put him above her dead siblings.

She was going to let them do it, she decided. Once Grandpa was out of the hospital, she would let her friends do what she could still not do herself. But before that, she needed to find a future for herself and her son.

CHAPTER 14

It was close to midnight when Ruston finally headed for home. But even though he knew he should be heading home, he was driving toward Hazel's house. Toward Hazel. It was late, and he would have to be home by seven in the morning, but he was willing to do anything to have her in his arms for a few hours.

All day she had been on his mind. After he had left her grandparents, he had gone down the hallway to visit another parishioner who was losing his battle with cancer. It had been a long, hard fight, and it showed on the man. His wife had asked Ruston to stay, and he had. There was no place he would rather be. Well, there was one place, but it would have to wait.

Once the man had died, Ruston had sat and prayed with his wife and kids. This was the part of the job he hated, but he always did it willingly. It was painful but rewarding.

Picking up his phone, he called Thomas as he drove. He needed someone to talk to.

"Why are you calling me so late? Are you out partying? It's Saturday night."

"No, I'm going home from the hospital. Cancer," Ruston told him.

"You?" Thomas sounded instantly awake.

"No, a parishioner," Ruston said quickly, hating that he had scared his friend like that.

"Lead with that, man," Thomas demanded.

"Next time, sorry," Ruston said, glad his friend was concerned about his health.

"So why are you calling at midnight?" Thomas relaxed into the call, it seemed.

"I needed to talk to someone."

"Your dad busy?" Thomas was right; he usually talked about the tough stuff with his dad. But this time, he didn't feel right about it.

"I don't want to talk to my dad about this."

"Sex?" Thomas asked, and Ruston could tell he was smiling. He was glad they were not in the same room because Thomas had a way of getting details from him others couldn't.

"Yes."

"About getting any or not getting any?" Thomas asked.

"Getting."

"Tell me that it's that hot little singer you had relations with over the summer."

"Nicely put."

"Answer."

"Yes, with her. She's been avoiding me for months, but yesterday her grandpa collapsed and was sent to the hospital. Her friend got me to go out to her farm."

"Forced you, I bet. You were fighting it the entire time," Thomas teased.

"Shut up. So anyway, things happened. Things I shouldn't have let happen." He was letting the guilt get to him about sleeping with her. He wanted to date her and, yes, sleep with her. But with his job, he knew he shouldn't be sleeping with her. And yet here he was, driving toward her place.

"Rusty, you're in a little town, and you're supposed to be asexual. It's hard when you're twenty-eight and have the hots for a sexy little woman." Thomas understood completely, even if he had never been in this type of situation. His love life was in the open for anyone to see.

"Very hard." He blew out a breath.

"Do you want me to forgive you? Do you want me to say way to go? Do you want me to tell you that you made a mistake?" Thomas asked.

"I want you to tell me that what I feel is real and that she feels it too. And maybe that it's okay."

"I will tell you what your dad would tell you: God has a plan for you, and you don't know what it is. You just have to go with it."

"She doesn't believe in God," he told his friend.

"From what you've said, she believes in him, she just thinks he's abandoned her. She doesn't see that God has a plan for her too. Hers is just harder than others. It'll make her stronger in the end," Thomas said. When Ruston needed real advice, Thomas was his man.

"You're good with advice. That's why I called you. Thanks," Ruston told him.

"I hope I helped. Say hi to Hazel when you get home." Thomas chuckled into the phone.

"How do you know I was going to see her?"

"Because I would be if it were me." Thomas was a player, so Ruston didn't really believe he would be settling for one woman. Not any time soon.

"I'm not going home; I'm going to her place."

"Ruston, home *is* her. You'll realize it soon enough." Thomas hung up on him. For a guy with a new girl on his arm every week, Thomas was quite the romantic.

Ruston quietly walked into the house, just then wondering if her grandma was home. The thought hadn't crossed his mind. What would she think of him sneaking into her granddaughter's bed in the middle of the night? That thought alone should send him home.

It might have if he hadn't spotted Hazel lying on the couch. She was reading a book with only a lamp for light. Well, she wasn't reading it anymore; it was lying over her chest as if she had fallen asleep reading it.

Quietly, he walked over to her. She looked younger and innocent, sleeping there. She was in a T-shirt and shorts in the warm house.

Picking up the book, he read the cover. 'Serial Killers' was all it said, and he looked back down at the innocent sleeping face. Closing the book, he thought maybe they should spend more time talking—he had no idea where her reading interests lay.

Carefully he picked her up into his arms. She was light and snuggled into him as he carried her up the stairs. Setting her in the bed, he pulled back the covers and slid her under them.

Glancing at John Henry, he reached into the crib and touched his head, touched the hair he had inherited from his mom. The boy was easy to love, like his mother. But John Henry was quick to return the love he was shown.

What he should've done was leave. She was sleeping, and he didn't want to disturb her. Instead, he stripped down to his underwear, carefully climbed into bed with her, and pulled her to him, so her body fit into his. Ruston let out a sigh. This was what he had been waiting for all day, just to feel her close to him.

CHAPTER 15

HAZEL HAD BEEN a little late getting to Ruth's house for book club. The day had gotten away from her, and John Henry had been crabby for most of it. Today would have been a day to have stayed in bed. Of course, she had thought about staying in bed all day when she had opened her eyes to see Ruston looking at her. The moment her eyes opened, he ran a finger over her cheek, like he had been waiting to do it for hours.

She had trailed her hand up his bare chest until it ran up his neck and into his hair. The sun had barely started to rise as she pressed her body to his and lifted her head to kiss his neck. He made a noise at her touch, and then his eyes went to John Henry on the other side of her.

Kissing up to his ear, she whispered, "Do you want to take a shower, preacher man?"

Without waiting for his answer, she got up and went to the bathroom. Had she thought he would say no, that he wouldn't follow her? That had never crossed her mind as she turned on the water and waited for it to get warm. Pulling off her T-shirt and shimmying out of her shorts and underwear, he came all sexy through the door and closed it behind him.

Forgetting about the water running in the shower, she went to him and pulled his head down for a kiss. It was hot and demanding and left her breathless as his arms wrapped around her and pulled her close to him.

Spinning, he lifted her and set her down on the vanity, his attention turning to her breasts, first one then the other, as her hands ran up his back and scratched down it.

"Haze, you're going to leave marks." His mouth nuzzled her neck.

"I don't care." She pushed his boxers down his legs and wrapped herself around him, urging him inside, needing him inside her.

"What about the shower?" He grabbed her hips and held her back from pulling him inside her.

"No time, I need you inside me now." She all but begged as her body ached for him.

"Fuck," he hissed and let go of her hips, meeting her halfway as he plunged into her.

Her head fell back, and she groaned at the sensation of him filling her. Exactly what she needed. Hands gripping the vanity, she let him do the work of driving them over the edge, letting him take control. Looking into his eyes, she saw he was looking behind her, at the mirror.

"Are you watching us, Ruston?"

His eyes focused on hers at her words. But she watched as the blue eyes turned back to the mirror. With effort, she unwrapped her legs from him and pushed him away. Confusion clouded his eyes. They were on her now. She slid off the counter and turned her back to him.

Spreading her legs, she said, "It'll be hotter this way."

Feeling him come up behind her as she watched, he kissed her shoulder as he slid easily back into her. His hands went around her hips as he started moving again. Faster this time.

Grabbing his hands, she slid them to her breast. With a moan, she leaned back and said, "Watch us, Ruston."

His eyes that had been on her moved up to the mirror as his movements picked up speed again, and he started to swear in rhythm with his movements. His hands slid back down to her hips as she watched, and an orgasm rippled through her body. He growled as he came, and she watched it happen.

They hadn't made it into the shower since the water was running cold before they got to it. But it had been worth it. The downside was that Ruston would have to leave earlier since he needed to shower and shave before church.

Hazel had gone down to make coffee and breakfast, and Ruston had gone to get his clothes from her room. But when he came down, he was carrying John Henry, who was up earlier than usual. Both of them realized that they had made too much noise in the bathroom and had woken the little boy. Hazel was glad they hadn't tried sex in the bedroom.

Afterward, Ruston had left. He had only asked her once to come to church while she and John Henry ate breakfast. She got her son dressed and let him play while she finally took a short, hot shower, but the water turned cold again. Still worth wasting the hot water that morning.

She didn't go to church, but she did force herself to go to the hospital to see her grandfather. Leaving John Henry with her grandmother, she went into the room. He was hooked up to beeping machines. Different from when she had seen the twins—there were no machines that night, just silence in death. She didn't say anything to the lifeless form. Just stood and looked down at him.

Memories washed over her. Before the accident, he had been loving and supportive, never with a negative word for his grandchildren. He had loved having the three kids around, teaching them everything he knew, learning new things to teach them. But after the accident, he had been cold and distant to the remaining one. Even more so after she came back with John Henry. Though he had never said he was disappointed in her, he had proved so with his actions.

Looking at him, she wished he would get better, wished he would come back as the grandfather who had raised her. The fun one who laughed. The one who had loved her.

Leaving him without a word, she returned to her grandmother and saw that John Henry was playing with the toy he had brought along in the corner, far away from her grandma. Leaving him to play, she sat down next to the woman. "How are you doing? Have you been sleeping?" she asked because they hadn't spoken in days.

"I'm as good as I can be. I sleep on and off."

"What do they say about him?" Hazel asked, not wanting to hear what the doctors said but needing to.

"The longer he doesn't wake up, the worse it will be."

"You should come home. You can't stay here all the time." Hazel didn't want her to come home, but she also didn't want her to be sleeping at the hospital and being uncomfortable.

"I'm not going back there." Her anger surprised Hazel.

"You can't stay away forever," Hazel told her. It was her home, after all.

"I've decided to move into the retirement home, no matter what happens with John." She was watching John Henry playing with his toys.

"What about the farm?"

"I talked to Ken Reed, and he's going to buy it. He's always shown an interest in the land. He's giving me a fair price, and it'll be enough for me to live on for years to come. It's all I can ask for." Her grandma didn't meet her eyes.

"Grandpa won't want to sell." Which was why he was still farming at his age. He wanted to be there.

"Your grandpa isn't going to be able to farm again," Rose hissed.

"And me?" she asked quietly, her future in her grandmother's hands.

"You're no farmer, Hazel. You've played at it for years now. Go and find something you are good at."

The old woman's word stung.

Hazel had put her life into that farm—everything she had put into being a farmer. They thought she was playing at it, not taking it seriously. They had seen the real her the entire time. They had seen that her heart wasn't in it.

"I have nothing," she whispered, but her grandmother didn't hear her. She hadn't even been paid for the job she had done, just room and board for her and her son. She had nothing—less than nothing.

"You'll have a month to get the house cleaned out. I'll come and take some of my clothes, and the rest is yours. Sell it or whatever," Rose May said.

Hazel leaned back in her chair and wondered what she was supposed to do next. She had no job, no home, and no skills. Getting up, she went to her son and picked up his toys and started to leave with him, but turned and asked, "Do you wish I had been in that accident too?"

Her grandmother looked up at her with cold eyes. "Don't make me talk about it."

Hazel left at the words. Hurrying out of the hospital, she got herself and her son situated in her yellow beetle and drove around town, wondering what to do next, where to go from there. Maybe Grand Forks? But she had no money for a down payment on an apartment, no job, and no one to watch her son.

Knowing it was book club night and that she should be coming back to town in a few hours, she headed home. Concentrating on feeding her son, she tried not to think about how she was going to feed him in a month.

As he played, Hazel started to go through things in her bedroom, throwing out what she didn't need. Since she had so little space, she usually threw things out as she stopped using them, but with her new future, she dug deeper and got rid of more stuff.

Her phone rang. She saw it was Ruston, and her heart sank. She needed to end it with him before someone found out about them. There was no future for them. Staying with her had been a danger to his career, so she let it ring, staring at the quiet phone after it stopped.

It immediately rang again, and again it was him. Sitting on her bed amongst her stuff, she answered. "Ruston, I'm glad you called. We need to talk." She tried to sound cheery, but she had to end it now.

"I stopped in to see your grandpa today. I heard you were there."

How soon after she left had he arrived? What did her grandmother tell him?

"I stopped by," was all she said, but he already knew.

"Good, you needed to see him in case he doesn't make it out of it."

"I'm at peace with him."

"Are you going to book club tonight?"

"No, I have to text Mia about that. I can't do book club right now." She couldn't do much anymore.

"You should go. It'll take your mind off everything. Even for a little while."

"I have no one to watch John Henry."

"I will."

Shaking her head, even if he couldn't see her, she said, "Ruston, no. He's my responsibility. Sometimes I don't get to do things because of him, but I'm okay with that."

"And I said I'm willing to watch him. Sometimes you have to accept help." His voice had an edge to it she wasn't used to.

"Ruston—"

"Just drop him off. We'll have a guy's night. You just enjoy yourself. You need that," Ruston said, the edge gone.

His words made her decide to do what he wanted. To enjoy herself one last time before her life changed.

After dropping John Henry off, she was late, and nobody even asked her why. They just let her sneak in as they talked about Natalie's new adventure. Taking her seat as they talked, she thanked Ruth for the drink she set in front of her. After eight months, everyone knew what the others drank.

Natalie was still talking to the others as she took a chair next to Hazel. But she stopped and said, "How are you, Haze? Who's watching Beckett tonight?"

"His name is still John Henry," Hazel argued.

"He's cuter as a Beckett." Natalie grinned.

"Is Natalie trying to change your child's name, Hazel?" Tess asked.

"I'm just trying it out. She named him after me," Natalie told the entire group.

"His middle name is Beckett. By mistake, I can tell," Hazel said to them all.

"I'm going to keep calling him that until everyone is calling him that." Natalie tapped on her computer.

Ruth handed out the headphones, and all talk about personal things stopped for the next two hours. Hazel was finally able to think about something other than her future for a while. So maybe it was to talk about murder, but it was not her future.

Pulling the headphones off, she ran her fingers through her short hair as Mia started to tell them about the local gossip she had learned lately. She seemed to know everything that was happening in town.

"And you …" She turned to Hazel, who hadn't really been paying attention. "I heard in church today that you and the pastor are getting along a little *too* well."

"You knew that, Mia," Tess said as she filled her wine glass.

"Of course, I knew that, Tess. But the person who told me shouldn't have known that," Mia replied to her friend.

"Who was it?" Mandy asked since they all went to the same church.

"I do not tell my sources, but you have to be a bit more discreet," Mia stated.

"You're right. I have to end it. It'll destroy his career," Hazel said the words out loud.

"End it? No, just be discreet. There's no need to end it," Mia insisted.

"No, I have to end it." She sipped her drink and added, "I have to stop coming to book club too."

"There's no quitting book club." Natalie slammed her computer shut.

"I have to. I won't have time or anyone to watch John Henry in two weeks. Grandma sold the farm, and I have to be out in a month."

"I have a place for you," Ruth jumped in.

"I can't do that to you, Ruth. I have no money to pay rent. I'll find something."

"I will not take that as your answer, Hazel. I have a place, and you need a place. I do not need the money. Once you get on your feet, we'll figure it out. Until then, you have a place to live, no matter what."

Everyone around the table seemed to agree.

"And if you need a job, I'm always looking for someone," Mia offered quickly.

"I have a teller position open at the bank if you're interested." Tess patted Hazel's arm as she offered.

"I waitressed during college, but it's been a long time." Hazel wondered how she had found such great friends. Why were they so nice to her?

"You don't forget how. But think about it for a few days," Mia said.

"I have a friend who runs a daycare. I can talk to her about John Henry. And I'm only part-time at the library for the next few weeks. I can watch him when I'm not working." Natalie toasted her with her glass.

"My niece Tasha can watch him. She isn't a daycare, but she has kids already. One is even close to John Henry's age. She would be happy to do it," Tess said.

Though Hazel hadn't met them yet, she had seen Tess's family, and her niece had a ton of kids—eight, to be exact.

"You guys are being too nice. I don't really deserve it," Hazel said to the group.

"Of course, you do. You're our Hazel. What would this group be like without you?" Tess asked.

Mia took over the conversation again as she remembered another hot piece of gossip she needed to tell everyone. Hazel felt better for the first time since talking to her grandma. Maybe she had a better future than she had originally thought, a place to stay and a job.

Tomorrow she would start packing and getting her life organized. Tomorrow her life would begin.

CHAPTER 16

IT DIDN'T TAKE LONG for book club to break up and Hazel to head back to Ruston's to pick up her son. She just needed to break whatever they were doing off and pick up her son. It wasn't dark yet as she pulled up in front of the house, but it was close to her son's bedtime.

Ruston met her at the door and pulled her into a kiss on the front step. Pushing him in to the cool interior, she let him continue the kiss. She could enjoy the kiss, even if she was going to end it.

Pulling her mouth from his, she was breathing heavily as she looked around the living room. John Henry was sitting on the couch staring at the TV; he hadn't even noticed she was there yet. The popcorn bowl on his lap was keeping him busy.

"How was book club?"

"Good."

"Whiskey and coke?" he asked.

"If you know, why do you ask?"

"Because I like to talk to you." He ran his thumb over her cheek.

She pushed him away. "We have to talk."

"I don't like when we have to talk. That usually means you don't want to talk to me anymore." He tried to pull her back to him.

She walked into his little house, sidestepping him. The furniture fit with his personality, in browns and tan colors. It looked comfortable, and she could see him here. She wished she could spend more time with him there.

"We have to stop this." She forced the words out.

"What is this?" he questioned.

"This. Us."

"Why?"

"Mia heard something at church. There's gossip."

"I don't care."

"You have to care. This could end your career."

He shook his head. "I don't think it will come to that."

"I don't want to be the reason you have to leave."

"If I leave, Hazel, I'm probably taking you and John Henry with me."

"You know there's no future in this."

"No, Hazel, I don't know that. I feel that there's a future in this. In us."

"Well, you're wrong. I have no place in your life." She stormed over and grabbed her son from the couch. Leaving the house, she thought he would say something, but he just watched her walk away. After getting her son in his car seat, she pounded the steering wheel with her fists a few times. He was so aggravating.

Turning the key, she was surprised that the car didn't start. Calming herself, she tried again—nothing. Quietly, she said sorry for beating on the car, and she tried again, but still nothing. Now what?

Getting out of the car, she thought about looking under the hood but had no idea what it even looked like under there. Circling the little yellow car, she turned to look at Ruston's house and saw him on the front porch, watching her.

"Car troubles?" he called to her, not leaving the porch.

"I'll call Mia for a ride. Or Natalie," she called back to him.

"Or you can just take mine, bring it back tomorrow." He had finally gotten off the porch and was pulling the passenger door open to get John Henry out of the car.

"I don't want to come back."

He grabbed her T-shirt in the front, bunching it in his hand as he pulled her to him with it. "Yes, you do." Then he kissed her. Not some light peck, but a kiss that said that he didn't want her to leave. And she didn't; she wanted to stay kissing him in his yard forever.

With everything she had, she pushed him away and pulled her son from his arms where Ruston was still holding him. "I will take it, but I shouldn't."

"I'll get my keys," he said but grabbed John Henry's car seat out of the yellow beetle first. "It's in the garage, so you'll have to come through the house."

Following him silently, she hoped that no one saw the kiss. In the garage, she watched as he put the car seat in the back of his gray SUV, then let him put John Henry in the seat. She loved her little car, always had, but it was a hassle with the two-door car. His car was so big.

He handed her the keys and pulled her into his arms, pulling her close so she could feel his entire body pressed to her. Letting her eyes drift shut, she let herself melt into his one more time. One last time. Feeling his breath on her ear, he whispered, "Stay."

"I can't. I told you," she whispered back, her resolve melting away as his hands roamed her body in the semi-dark garage. She pulled away from him before he could kiss her again.

Closing the door, she started the car and backed out of the garage. The drive home was too short, and soon she was back in the empty house. Turning on every radio she could find, she filled the house with music. She needed music tonight.

With John Henry playing in their bedroom, she grabbed a garbage bag and opened the door to Hanna's room. The time was now. She had to do it in the next month anyway. Walking into the room, she saw the dust first—it covered everything, the dresser, the floor. Her sister wasn't coming back here.

After throwing out all the clothes and shoes, she took an open book off the bed. It felt odd closing it after all these years. Should she have put a bookmark in it? No. Nobody needed to know what page it had been on for all these years.

Removing the dusty bedding from the bed, a cloud of dust sent her from the room so it could settle. Back in the room, Hazel started on the books and papers on the desk. As she sat on the chair, John Henry came into the room and sat on her lap. Pulling open drawers, she threw away pens, pencils, and little things that meant nothing to anyone. A pile of hair ties, brochures for colleges she never went to, folders containing papers she had written for school classes, all thrown in the garbage bag.

A pile of pictures caught her attention, and she picked them up. She didn't remember where the pictures were taken, but it looked like a party somewhere sometime in the summer based on the clothes they were wearing. The top picture was Hanna and Natalie making peace signs at the camera.

John Henry pointed to the picture and said, "Mommy."

Pulling her son closer, she said, "No honey, that's Hanna."

"No, it's Mommy and Natalie."

Flipping through the pictures, she found one with her in it. "See, this is mommy. This is Hanna. She looks like me." She had never realized that her son had never seen a picture of Hanna. Did he even know who her sister was?

Flipping through more of the pictures, she found what she was looking for. "This one is Henry. You were named after him." Putting that picture beside the one with her and Hanna, she added, "We were three."

John Henry held up four fingers, and she put one of them down. "Three."

She hugged the little boy to her as she fought the tears. Her son didn't even know her siblings. She had somehow thought about them every day but never talked about them. The most important person in her life was unaware of her identical twin and brother, who hung over her family.

When the boy fought his way out of her arms, she let him go, and he took the pile of pictures with him as he left. Turning back to the desk, she pushed through to get it done. Once the desk was empty, she took the posters off the walls and the floor where some had landed through the years.

After filling another bag, she put it in the hallway with the other two she had filled. Turning back to the room, it looked so different now than an hour before. The only thing left was the schoolbook. She would give it to Natalie to give to Sam. She picked it up to take it downstairs so she would remember.

Once back upstairs, she turned to Henry's room. This one was easier. Once the clothes, shoes, and bedding were gone, she easily cleared his desk. He was not a saver and had thrown a lot of the things that had cluttered Hanna's desk. There were no pictures or keepsakes for her brother. Removing the knickknacks from on top of the dresser, she stopped. Slowly, she picked up the piece of dusty paper containing her son's name written in her brother's handwriting and blew the dust off it, then took it and put it on the book on the dining room table.

Looking at the clock, she realized it was almost midnight. She hadn't even put John Henry to bed yet. Back upstairs, she went looking for him and found him sleeping in her bed with the pictures scattered around him. He was holding the one of her and Hanna as he slept. Since they were all laid out around him, she picked out the ones with Natalie and her sister or brother and put them in a pile for her friend. The rest she put in another pile. She would put them in an album one day. One day when she was settled into her new life.

Taking the last picture from his hand, she went downstairs to look for a frame to put it in for her son. Tomorrow, she would start talking about her siblings to her son so he would know them too.

Since John Henry was in her bed, she decided to sleep on the couch and not disturb the boy. She fell asleep looking at her and her sister smiling into the camera, not knowing their time together was so short. Not realizing the futures they wanted were not guaranteed.

CHAPTER 17

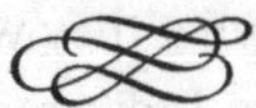

A FAINT POUNDING on his front door woke Ruston up from a deep sleep. Instinctively, he reached out for Hazel before remembering that she wasn't beside him. After just two nights with her, he was already used to her being there and missed her when she wasn't.

When the pounding came again, he got out of bed and realized what had woken him. Grabbing his phone from the bedside table, he checked it for missed calls. Since there was nothing, he had no idea what was going on. Who needed him enough to show up at his house? Walking to the door, he thought maybe he should change out of his sweatpants and T-shirt but dismissed the idea since they were at his door at 7:00 a.m. If someone needed to see him so early, they would have to take him as he was.

Swinging the door open, he saw Patrick Beckett and Sam Sullivan on his front step. Neither man looked happy to be there, and he had no idea what they could want so early. Patrick was Natalie's dad, and Sam was her fiancé.

Instantly, he was worried about the young woman. "Is something wrong with Natalie?"

Patrick shook his head, then asked, "Can we come in? Do you have company?"

"Come on in," he replied in confusion, but if the men needed to talk, he was there for them.

Stepping back, both men walked into the house, both looking around. Though he was sure neither had been to his house, he saw both their eyes looking into the other rooms they could see.

"Is Hazel here?" Patrick asked, his eyes coming back to rest on Ruston.

"No." He wondered again what they were doing here.

"Her car is out front." Sam indicated through the window at the yellow beetle.

It was still parked in front of his place; he hadn't even looked at it after she left, deciding to wait until morning to even try. No use looking in the dark. But now, based on the men's demeanor, they might be the talk of the town.

Angrily, he realized Hazel had been correct to be worried. He should have known that it would take just one night for the town to start talking, but he had naively thought they could remain in the bubble they had at the farm. A bubble he had hated to leave, hated to hide.

Crossing his arms, he didn't like what they were saying. "I watched John Henry so she could go to book club. Then the car didn't start, so she took mine home. She's not here. If you need to search the house, you can."

"No need for that," Sam said, seeming embarrassed to even be there as he sat down on the couch.

"There are rumors going around that you and Hazel are having an inappropriate relationship," Patrick stated and sat down in the armchair across from his future son-in-law.

"I don't think that my relationship with Hazel is any of your business, or anyone else's for that matter," Ruston said, sitting up straighter.

Patrick shook his head. "Ruston, your relationship with Hazel is none of my business. In fact, I think you would make her happy. But as a preacher, you have a reputation to maintain."

Ruston looked at the older man, who was currently living with his girlfriend and her kids, and Sam was living with his fiancé. Neither was married to the women they lived with. And they were here to talk to him about what was happening with Hazel? That they had spent one night together? Or that the entire town thought that they had spent one night together?

"So, because I am a preacher, I cannot date?" he asked. In the years he had lived in Landstad, he hadn't dated much and never here in town. Mostly because he hadn't met anyone he was that interested in. But he knew one day he would. Because he wanted to date Hazel, he wanted everything with Hazel.

"Of course, you can date. You just can't stay the night. Or at least have people know you're staying the night," Patrick said with a wink.

"Does it bother you that I stayed the night?" he asked Patrick, who was a member of his church.

"No, but I'm not one who's ever cared about that. There are others that will look at it differently than I do," Patrick answered, not meeting his eyes.

"And you?" he asked Sam.

He didn't know Sam very well; he had just started to attend services with Natalie. And though he knew Natalie fairly well, he hadn't had more than a conversation or two with Sam.

"If I had an issue with it, I would have said something the other day when her grandpa ended up in the hospital." Sam leaned back on the couch. He wasn't there to chastise him; he had just been roped into being there. Though Ruston had no idea why.

"What do you expect me to do?" Ruston asked them.

"That depends on what you want," Patrick said. "If she's nothing but a good time, dump her and do not speak to her again. It'll all be over soon when there's nothing new happening. But if you love her, I suggest marrying her and marrying her quickly. The rumors are going to get worse before they go away."

"We just started whatever this is we're doing. I don't want to move too quickly with her. And at this point, she would never agree to marry me." Ruston ran his hands over his face. Last night, she had all but said it was over. She would not marry him today. He had known they'd lost steps in their journey that he would have to get through again.

"Are you in love with her?" Sam's words surprised him. Thomas had asked almost the exact same question.

"Yes. But she's hesitant about a relationship with me, which means we're taking it slowly."

"Do you want a relationship with her?" Sam rephrased his question.

"Of course. I want to spend the rest of my life with her. But I can't push her to do what she isn't ready for. I in no way want to pressure her. Being with me has to be her decision. Her choice. I have to put in the time and energy to convince her we belong together." Didn't these two men see how fragile Hazel was? How protective of her heart she was?

The two men looked at each other and seemed to be deciding something right there. Was it about his future at the church? Were they realizing that they needed to fire him? Suspend him?

Patrick turned back to him. "I have known Hazel her entire life, and I love the girl to pieces, but I also know that she isn't as fragile as you think she is. Nothing in her life has broken her, and there has been plenty that could have."

"I don't want to force her. If she wants me, I will wait. She's worth any amount of time I have to wait." It was true. She was the one for him, and he was going to put in the necessary time.

"I don't know if you have that kind of time. There's gossip going around that she's leading you astray. After all, she has a son and no dad in sight. Some of the older crowd doesn't think she's the type of woman you should be messing around with. And if you get enough people talking, your job might be at risk," Patrick said.

Blowing out a breath, he asked, "I'm the same person I was when they hired me. Still single. Don't they want me to get married?"

"Of course, they do, but a few of the old biddies have an issue with a single mom. And I'm sad to say the longer they talk about it, the more they'll convince others that what you're doing is wrong."

Sam looked at his friend. "Patrick is right. Time is of the essence here."

"She needs time, and I can't force her to do something she doesn't want to or isn't ready for."

"I think you can. Force her, that is," Patrick said, not even pretending he wasn't talking about forcing the woman to do something she didn't want to do.

"Excuse me?" Ruston sat up.

"I know that sounds bad, very bad. But in high school, Hanna and Natalie always got her to do what they wanted her to do by bullying her. Well, it wasn't really bullying; it was more saying she couldn't do whatever. It always spurred her into doing it, whether she wanted to or not. I'm assuming those tactics will still work. And use everything you have over her."

Ruston wondered if he knew the woman at all. Or had she changed that much in the last few years? "I don't think I can do that to her," Ruston argued. Not the Hazel he loved.

"Then cut her loose," Patrick said.

"Natalie said that her grandparents have sold the farm. Hazel has a month to get the house clean and move out. The book club is working on getting her a job and an apartment, but they all think she'll go to Grand Forks and leave here for good. Can you live with that?" Sam said as the men got up and walked out, leaving Ruston alone in his thoughts.

How was he going to get Hazel to marry him? Because letting her go was not an option. After all, she had been a part of him since that early summer party.

Now there was a possibility that he wouldn't have her, that she was going to leave, and his time would be up. He wasn't ready for that.

CHAPTER 18

By 9:00 A.M., he had showered and gotten her car started—a loose wire had been the issue, so it had been an easy fix. Now he was outside her door, still wondering what he was going to say. How was he going to get her to agree to be his wife?

The house was unusually silent as he opened the door. By this time of the day, she was up and had the radio on with John Henry running around the house, but neither was moving. Near the front door, there were some garbage bags sitting by the wall.

Looking into the kitchen, he saw nothing. Then he quietly walked up the stairs to her room. On his way past, he saw the other doors were open, and the rooms were cleaned out. Just furniture was left. Had she done this last night? She had to have since he had been there that morning. Looking into Hazel's bedroom, he saw John Henry lying in her bed. His eyes were open, but he hadn't been up long based on his tired, heavy eyes.

The little boy saw him and smiled. "Ruston." Then jumped up and threw himself into Ruston's arms.

"Where's your mommy?" he asked the little boy, who didn't answer.

Going back downstairs, he finally found her sleeping on the couch, still in the clothes she had worn the night before. The night must have been late for these two. The amount of work she had done would have taken hours. Setting the boy down, he went to the kitchen and started to make breakfast for the two of them.

As he started to make pancakes, John Henry came and handed him a picture frame. Taking it, he put it on the counter. The faces that looked back at him were smiling and so similar it hurt to look at them. John Henry pointed to the picture and said, "Mommy and Hanna."

"I know, buddy. Aren't they cute?"

"Do you know which is mommy?" John Henry asked, holding the photo an inch from Ruston's face.

Ruston pulled the picture away and looked at it closely. There were slight differences in the two that people would be able to tell them apart, but for him, it was a feeling. He knew the one on the left but not the one on the right. "This one." He pointed to that one.

"How do you know that's me?" Hazel asked from the doorway, her voice husky from sleep.

Turning, he saw that though she was awake, she still looked tired. With her hair messed from sleep and her clothes wrinkled, she was still beautiful. "Because I'm in love with that one, and I don't know the other."

"You're not in love with me, Ruston. You just like to fudge me," she protested with a grin at her camouflaged wording.

"I do like to fudge you, but I also love you." He tried to pull her into his arms, but she stepped back from him.

"I'm going to change. Thank you for feeding him. Did you fix my car?"

"Yes, loose wire. Shouldn't be an issue anymore."

Then she was gone, and he heard her footsteps going up the stairs, He realized that her bedroom was over the kitchen when he heard her opening and closing dresser drawers. John Henry helped him make the pancakes, and Ruston watched as the boy ate more of them than he had ever expected.

As John Henry ate, he looked at the picture. He chatted about it.

He was amazed there was another that looked just like his mom. When he was done eating, he wordlessly took the picture with him as he left the table.

Soon Hazel was coming down the stairs with a different pair of jeans on and an old Garth Brooks concert T-shirt. Her attitude had not improved with her shower. In fact, it had gotten worse. The more awake she was, the angrier she was.

When she got to the dining room, she tossed her phone on the table and said, "Natalie texted 'things are happening.' People are talking a lot."

"I know, we have to talk."

"You just take your car and go home. I'll keep low for a while, and it will blow over." Her words mirrored the ones said in his living room a few hours before.

He knew she was right, but he didn't want to leave her. He never wanted to leave her. "I don't know if it'll be that easy. I think it's gone too far." He began to take Sam's advice.

"Are they going to fire you?" she asked, her eyes wide with concern.

"Probably," he lied. He hated doing this to her.

"I can talk to them. I'll say you stayed on the couch, that nothing happened." He could see her mind racing, coming up with a story everyone would believe.

"They won't believe you," he insisted.

"Who's on the board? I know them, I'm sure. I can get them to listen to me."

"No, Hazel. They've given me two options." He did not want to do this. Lying to her was the last thing he ever wanted to do to her.

"What are they?" She sat down in empty John Henry's chair.

"I can leave, or we can get married." He full-out lied to the woman he loved, and he hated it.

"Where will you go?" Her words were forced, and he hoped she wasn't going to have a panic attack. Until that moment, he hadn't even thought about it.

Quickly, he steered the conversation to staying here. "I want to stay in Landstad. This is my home. Which means that I think we should get married."

"I can't be a preacher's wife," she stated firmly.

"If I leave, it will be on my record." He had no idea what he was talking about.

"So, it will follow you forever?" She chewed on her lip as she thought about it.

"Yes," he lied again, sitting in the chair closest to her, working at not touching her.

"But I don't want to marry you," she said with little conviction. Was it that easy to change her mind? To get her to do what she didn't want to do just minutes ago?

"We can go today and get a ring. Make it official." He ignored her words completely and pushed on.

"I don't think it will work." She was now pacing the room, turning every few feet because the room wasn't very big.

"We can visit my parents while we're in Grand Forks." Again, he didn't actually answer the question and pushed more.

Her feet were still moving across the room, back and forth, back and forth. But they were slowing. "They won't like me," she insisted, running her fingers through her short hair.

"I wish I could see what you see when you look at yourself. They're going to love you and John Henry."

"What will people say?" she asked, stopping completely.

"That we're excited to get married. I think two weeks from Saturday." It wasn't that far away, but the less time she had to think about it, the better.

"What?"

"One week from Saturday? This needs to happen fast, or nobody will believe it," he lied, knowing they could be engaged for years, and nobody would say anything. Except she wouldn't marry him if she knew they could put it off for months.

"No, that's too soon. Three weeks," she argued, pulling out her phone to look at the calendar.

"Three weeks from last Saturday." He pulled her onto his lap. "You will be mine."

She shook her head at the phone. "What? That's only two and a half weeks. How am I going to do that?"

"That's what God gave you a book club for."

"Book club is for murder only." She pushed off his lap and out of his arms with a frown.

Getting up, he followed her as she walked out of the kitchen. "They're your best friends. Now go put on something you haven't owned since high school, and I'll see if my parents want to meet you today."

"Don't you work?" she asked, stopping in the doorway.

"Day off."

She shrugged before leaving the room and heading upstairs. He listened to her footsteps go up the stairs again and smiled at the sound. Bullying works. He would be more bothered by it if she hadn't just agreed to marry him in less than a month's time. And he promised himself to never do it again.

Glancing in the living room, he saw John Henry playing quietly, so he went out onto the porch and dialed his mom. After she greeted him in her usual warm manner he said, "Hi, Mom. How are you?"

"Great, my favorite son is calling me."

Ruston laughed at the running joke that all her kids were her favorite as long as they were the ones talking to her. "I didn't realize Jack was even there."

His mom laughed. "You know me so well. Why are you calling me on your day off?"

"I was wondering if you and Dad would be home this afternoon?" His dad was a minister who had the day off as well. It was the day he usually went to visit them since they were both home.

"As far as I know. I'll make your father stay home. Is there a special reason you want to see us?" she pressed.

"Do you want me to tell you now or wait so I can say it in person?"

She paused and pondered the question. "Tell me now, and I won't tell your dad. You can surprise him. Have you met someone?"

"Yes, Mom, and we're getting married in around three weeks. I want you to meet her and her son," he said, knowing his mom was not going to be able to hide the information from his father, even for a few hours. His mom would have to tell someone, and that someone was his dad.

"Why so soon? Love?" his mom questioned with interest.

"I don't want to give her time to think about it," he said, not answering the love question.

"What's her name? Do I know her?" his mom asked.

"No, you don't know her. But you will. It's Hazel May. May is her last name." It always sounded like he was calling her by her middle name when he said her whole name. Maybe that's why he sometimes did.

"What, Hazel? Is that the one Thomas has been teasing you about for a few months?" His mom missed nothing. And Thomas wasn't known for his secret-keeping skills.

"Yes," he admitted.

"Thomas is usually right about these things. Come when you get to town. We'll be ready."

He had no idea what she did to get ready. She loved guests and was already ready. "Mom, just you and Dad. No brothers today," he said, knowing his mom might just call all five of his brothers home and freak Hazel out.

"Okay, this time."

Hanging up on his mom, he was still smiling when he got a text from an unknown number. All it said was congrats, so he assumed it was from Natalie since he had just given her his number yesterday.

CHAPTER 19

Ruston's parents were loving and accepting, hugging Ruston, then her, and even John Henry before they had even learned their names. They were exactly what she would have pictured if someone had asked her what they would be like. Hazel had been surprised for a moment when he had said his father was also a preacher, but it made sense. It also made sense that his mom would immediately take John Henry from her with a promise of cookies.

The woman was chatty and happy, making Hazel feel comfortable. More comfortable than she ever should have felt here. After all, Ruston was all but forced to marry her. And if he didn't, he might lose his job. She never wanted to be the reason he lost his job.

They hadn't been anything but excited and congratulatory when Ruston had told them they were getting married. Even when he had said they were getting married in a few weeks. They made it seem like it wasn't unusual for things to happen so quickly.

Once the men ate the cookies, Ruston's dad took him off to his office to show him something, leaving Hazel alone with his mom. Based on the glares Ruston gave his parents, this wasn't planned at all. She was sure he was going to get a lecture from his dad.

Sitting down at the table with John Henry, who was already eating his second cookie, his mom handed her a coffee and sat down with them. It was a little too cozy for Hazel. She wasn't used to parental figures wanting to talk to her. After all, her grandparents hadn't been all that talkative.

"You sure do make Rusty happy," his mother Joan said with a smile that was so much like her son's. Hazel would have to get used to him being called Rusty, even if he didn't seem like a Rusty.

"Thank you. He's a happy guy. Gets it from you guys." Hazel took a sip of the bitter coffee, really hoping she was impressing the woman but thinking she was failing.

"All of my boys are generally happy. I don't know if Glen and I had anything to do with it," she admitted with a shrug.

"How many boys do you have?" Ruston hadn't said anything about having siblings, and now she realized she hadn't asked. In fact, there was so little she had asked about his life. How could he know so much about her, but she know so little about him?

"Six. Rusty said I couldn't invite them over today. But next time." There was a twinkle in the woman's eyes.

"That sounds like a lot of people," Hazel admitted, looking around the room and imagining it filled with Ruston's family.

"You get used to it. You only have one. When there are more, they get a lot noisier." She smiled at John Henry.

"Do you mind that I have a son?" she asked, not knowing what his mom thought about it.

Had Ruston told his family about her past? Did they know that John Henry had no father, that he had never had a father?

"Of course not. I'll love him like all my other grandkids. We don't treat the children any different."

"You are very understanding, Mrs. Abbott."

"Harris, but please call me Joan. Ruston's dad was my first husband. Glen Harris is my second. My boys kept their dad's name when I married," Joan explained, which surprised Hazel. Ruston had never said anything about his dad not being his real dad. But then again, maybe he didn't even think about it.

"Ruston never said anything about that." Hazel started to clean the crumbs John Henry had made on the counter.

Joan stopped her and cleaned it herself with a smile. "I don't know if he thinks about it. He was three when I married, around John Henry's age. I had four boys, and Glen had two. So, together we have six."

"How did you meet?" she asked.

Joan sat back down and took a sip of her coffee before saying, "He was a visiting preacher at the church I attended, and he caught my eye before the service. We chatted for a bit, and he actually asked me out. With four kids, right there. Then, during the service, my Rusty and Randy started running and screaming during the sermon. Glen was able to catch one of them, but Rusty ran around the entire time. And he still took me out for lunch after. We got married soon after."

"I would have hauled John Henry out of there if it had been us. Probably never going back again," Hazel admitted.

"Glen got to see what he was getting into, and he still wanted to be a part of it. To this day, I can't tell you why, but I'm happy about it." Joan grinned behind her coffee cup.

Maybe she and Ruston's mom had something in common, that they were ending up with men they didn't think they deserved. Except she assumed Joan was the perfect minister's wife, something Hazel knew nothing about.

"Are you telling stories about me, Mom?" Ruston walked into the room with a tall, dark-haired man. A brother? Though they looked nothing alike, he could be a stepbrother.

"Good to see you, Thomas," Joan said to the man and jumped up to give him a hug.

"Hi, Ruston's mom. Are you ready to adopt me yet?" The man joked with Joan and kissed her on the top of her head.

"I think your mom would be upset if I did." Joan laughed.

"Hazel, this is my friend, Thomas Harstad. My best friend since I was three." Ruston introduced her to the man, though he had wrapped an arm around her as he did.

"Before or after you almost destroyed your mom's chances with Glen?" Hazel teased him.

"After." He smiled and kissed the top of her head. "Thomas is going to be my best man."

"Nope, I'm going to marry you two. You're not so special, Ruston. I can marry people too. And since she'll probably want to get married in your church, and you can't do it, I will." Thomas spun a chair around, straddled it, and sat between the women.

"I guess I have to look for a best man then," Ruston said with a laugh.

"You will never find a better man than me, but good luck trying." He had barely been sitting a minute when he quickly got up and put the chair right. "Nice to meet you, Hazel. I've been waiting to meet you for a while now. But I only took an hour off, so I have to get back to work."

"Nice to meet you too, Thomas." She shook his hand and tried to catch her breath. He was nothing but movement.

"Just want to tell you that you have a beautiful voice," he said and left the room.

Hazel's eyes met Ruston, and her eyes went wide. Thomas was at the party. Did he remember her? Did he know what happened after she sang? Had Ruston told him? She could feel her cheeks turning red and saw Ruston watching with amusement in his eyes.

"Mom, can you watch John Henry so I can take Hazel out to eat and buy her a ring?" Ruston asked. It was something they hadn't discussed. Mostly because she had no idea what this trip was going to entail. And as long as she could ignore the entire wedding, the better.

"Of course, I'll spoil him rotten." Joan picked up the boy and rested him on her hip. John Henry went willingly and without even noticing it was nearly a perfect stranger holding him.

"Good. I don't know when we'll be back," Ruston called as he pulled Hazel out of the house. Hazel tried to protest leaving her son but stopped when he didn't even notice she was leaving him alone with strangers. But were they strangers? They were going to be his grandparents, after all.

The first stop had been the jewelry store, where Ruston spent too much on a ring that she loved. She tried to protest, saying he was spending too much since they still had to plan the wedding. He wouldn't listen and had her wear it out of the store.

Next, they went to a restaurant that Hazel had never heard of for a late lunch. Once they had ordered, Ruston took her hands in his and looked at her new ring. "I love your ring, Hazel. Do you like it?"

"You know I do. The book club says it's nice." She had texted them while they drove to the restaurant. Well, first, she texted them that she had agreed to marry him. Then had texted a picture of the ring because she had to show someone.

"Only nice?"

"*Very* nice." Hazel smiled.

"I love when I get to see that dimple."

She put her hands over her cheeks. She'd always hated her dimple.

"Did Hanna have a dimple?"

"Yes, we were identical. Everything was the same." She grinned because the boob incident with Natalie in high school popped into her mind.

"Are the girls getting everything ready for the wedding?"

"They're starting the process. I don't know what to do. Natalie is an expert, though." She hoped that it wouldn't be as elaborate as her wedding had been. If so, she might go through the window just to avoid everything.

"That she is," Ruston agreed.

The waiter came to their table and said, "Champagne from the table over there."

Hazel looked at the bubbly glass and then glanced over to where the waiter indicated and did a double-take. Ruston was sitting at another table with a red-haired woman, but she was sure he was still sitting across from her.

"Shit," Ruston muttered as the couple came over. Most of the time when he let swear words fly, she loved it. But not today.

"I told him to leave you alone, Rusty. He doesn't listen to me," the long-haired redhead said.

"Hazel, this is Ashley, who is Thomas's sister and also married to my brother Randy. Mom told you?" Ruston got up and hugged the woman, and even the man before Hazel had to be hugged by them as well.

"That she did." Randy looked at Hazel's shocked face. "Did you tell her you have a twin?"

"No, I didn't. I didn't think I would see him," Ruston said through gritted teeth.

"Sorry, Rusty," Ashley said again and patted him on his back.

"Are you okay, Hazel?" He squeezed the hands. Her mind was racing. Why had he never told her? The topic came up all the time.

"I'm sorry I didn't say anything," Ruston said, his fingers rubbing her hands, trying to calm her.

Ashley squatted down next to her chair and rubbed her back. "It's a shock, I know. They do look a lot alike. I don't notice it since I've known them my entire life."

"It's not that, Ash. She also had a twin," Ruston told her.

"It's okay, just a shock. I've never been on the other end of the twin surprise." Hazel breathed, calming herself. Calm breaths.

Not that she and Hanna had many opportunities to surprise people. They had rarely left town, and everyone there knew them. Looking back on it, she didn't think it was something they had ever done. Even trading places had been rare.

"Maybe we can have some twin surprises at the wedding. Two sets in one place," Randy said with a smile and rested his hand on his wife.

Hazel pulled her hands from Ruston's and put them on her lap. "My twin is dead."

"I'm sorry." Ashley hugged her, despite her turning completely bristly toward them.

These people were too friendly. She was sad, but she knew she wouldn't cry at the mention of Hanna. Randy and Ashley pulled up chairs and ordered when the waiter came by. Having dinner with his brother was fun. Randy loved to tease Ruston about everything, and Ashley had known them all their lives. Hazel just took it in and let them handle the conversation.

"So, Mom says you have a son?" Randy asked her with interest.

"Yes, John Henry is four," she told him.

"Where you twelve when you had him?" Ashley asked and punched her lightly in the shoulder.

"No, I was twenty. I don't look that young," Hazel argued. Yes, she was always carded, but she was not that young-looking.

"Keep telling yourself that," Ashley said. "I had my first at nineteen, and now I look like I have three and am also raising his guy." She pointed at her husband.

"Hey. I *am* raised. My mom made sure of it," Randy said to his wife in mock anger.

"No, you're not," Ashley told him with a grin.

Just then, Ruston got a phone call and excused himself as the couple continued to argue with each other. As Randy was pointing out how great he was in the kitchen, he got a text.

"Sorry, Hazel, we have to go. Tell Rusty that we love you, and he cannot let you go." Hazel watched him get up quickly and pull his shocked wife away from their half-eaten meal on the table and then out the door. Outside the window, she saw Ashley start yelling at him. He was going to get it.

She had found she liked Ruston's twin, though they were nothing alike besides the obvious. She was happy her twin was the better of the two. Turning away from the door, she saw him coming toward her. His eyes had lost the humor they had during the conversation with his family.

Once at the table, he said, "Let's go, Haze. We have to get back."

Panic set in immediately. "John Henry?"

"No, he's fine. Let's go."

Pulling her to the car, she ran through everything that could possibly be wrong. What had happened? Was it something with the gossip going around? Had it gotten even worse while they were gone? Because they were gone together?

Once in the car, Ruston turned to her. "Hazel, your grandfather died about an hour ago."

All she could do was nod at him. She knew it was a matter of time. She had said her goodbyes.

"Am I supposed to cry?" she asked as he pulled out of the parking lot.

"Do what you feel like doing," he said.

"I knew he wasn't getting better. And he had no will to live anymore. Not for years." She looked out the window. "I've realized in the last few weeks that we were all just living in that house, but none of us were alive."

"Do you want to be alive?" he asked.

"I don't know how to be," she admitted.

"Getting out of that house will help." He pulled up to his parents' house and went in to get John Henry, leaving Hazel in the car by herself.

She willed herself to cry over her grandfather who had just died. But she saw him as two men now: one who raised her with love and patience, and one who she moved back in with when she needed help and support and got little of either.

Back on the road, she watched the fields roll by for mile after mile. Ruston held her hand as he drove.

"Why did you clean the rooms last night?"

"I was a little drunk, and it needed to get done. I have a month before I have to move out."

"Weren't your friends going to help?" She hadn't told him that, so Natalie must have. Their conversations were letting him know too much.

"I had to do it myself. I needed to." Now that it was done, she did feel better. Though she felt that they weren't as close as they used to be—she had put distance between herself and her siblings, distance that was needed but never wanted.

"Did you learn anything?" he asked.

"Just that there was nothing really worth saving. They weren't in there anymore." She looked at the ring on her finger as she spoke.

"They're still with you, always."

She let the words float around the car, bringing her peace. They had never been in those rooms, but now she knew they weren't in her life either. And she wanted them in her life.

"I learned that John Henry didn't know them. I think about them every day, but I've never talked to him about them. I haven't kept their memories alive." She felt the tears she couldn't cry for her grandfather slip from her eyes.

CHAPTER 20

OF COURSE, the sun would shine the morning of John May's funeral. It couldn't rain and be gloomy—it had to be a beautiful, sunny day. Sitting in his office, he looked up at his bookshelf, at Hazel's boots that still sat there, months later. But now he also had Hazel. In just over two weeks, she would be his.

Ruston had expected her to cancel the wedding and maybe even stop the engagement, but the book club had pushed her to just keep on track. Knowing that they were doing most of the work had put Ruston's mind at ease that Hazel wasn't under too much pressure.

Getting up, he wanted to go sit with Hazel in the front row and hold her hand when she cried, but he had to officiate. Knowing she would have Natalie beside her made him feel a little better.

Walking out of his office, he saw the family gathering: Hazel, John Henry, and her grandma. Natalie was talking to her dad nearby. Hazel was wearing a black dress she must have borrowed from Tess or Ruth since it was a little big on her. Now that everyone knew they were engaged, Ruston was able to go up to Hazel and pull her into his arms for a hug. "How are you?"

"Good, I think," she said quietly into his chest.

Letting her go, he reached for her grandma's hand, but instead of shaking it, she pulled it away and turned from him. There was one person not happy for her granddaughter, but he wasn't going to let that bring them down.

When they entered the sanctuary, Rose told Ruston that she wanted Hazel to sing. That was all she said.

As he drew closer to the front of the church, he turned to Hazel and hugged her in front of the entire congregation without a second thought, whispering, "She wants you to sing."

"Okay," she whispered back, as if she hadn't heard what he had said.

"Which one?" He pulled away.

"Any of them." She mindlessly sat down.

Glancing over the songs, he decided which one it would be as he talked about all the good things he knew and had heard about the man they were burying today. When it was time, he announced that Hazel was going to sing. Murmurs floated through the church as she slowly got up. When she got to the front of the congregation, he picked up the guitar the other singer had left there.

It seemed like she was taking hours to straighten the instrument and make sure the straps were the right length. Shorten it, then it was too short, then too long again, then she took off the strap altogether, tucking it was between her body and the instrument.

She strummed the strings and tightened one, then did it again. Satisfied, she took a deep breath, looked at her fingers, and started to play the opening lines of Amazing Grace.

Once she started to sing, she stopped playing the instrument altogether and sang acapella. But she didn't lift her face, just looked at her fingers resting on the strings. Her voice was steady, sure, and simply amazing. He had heard the song hundreds of times in his life, but it had never moved him like when Hazel sang it.

When she finally sang the last verse, she set the guitar she had barely used back on its stand and walked shakily back to her seat. Wiping his eyes, he stood up and saw that people were either wiping their own tears away or just staring at the front.

"Thank you, Hazel. That was beautiful." He was looking at her and caught her eye, but they were clear of tears. It was surprising how she hadn't been able to shed many tears for her grandfather when tears were always at the surface with her.

Once the funeral was over, Ruston was outside in the sunshine to bury the man. Hazel would not attend this part; she had told him as much the night before. Her grandmother had been mad at her for not being with the woman for this important part, but it was what Hazel wanted, and he did not push it.

Now that the friends and few family members had left the folding chairs to go back in for lunch, Ruston sat on one of the chairs and prayed. Closing his eyes, he prayed that Hazel was not just pushing the pain of John's passing down only to come up when she least expected it. Though he had started to suspect that the years since the accident had changed the older couple and Hazel wasn't as close to them as she used to be. Even if they lived together.

With a deep breath, he decided he better get back in the church to be at Hazel's side where he belonged. And now that his duties were done, he could just be by her for support.

As he got up from the chair, he sat back down heavily. Right there was Hanna and Henry's grave. No wonder she didn't come out there. They were here, but where else would they have been? He wanted to laugh since Hanna's middle name was Hazel. And Hazel's middle name was Hanna. It was right there on her grave. A sudden anger rushed through his body that he had never felt before. He wanted to walk into that church and yell at the old woman until she finally realized how cruel she had been. Because instead of two names on the grave, there were three. The old couple had bought a grave for their granddaughter who had survived. In a way, telling her they would have liked her dead also.

"I don't know if she actually knows," Natalie said softly from behind him.

"How could she not know?" he demanded. His anger was focused on the wrong person. Because Natalie would never have done this to her friend.

"Because I don't think she's ever been out here." Natalie walked up beside him.

"Why would they even do this?"

"I wish I knew. I almost died in that accident, but Hazel has been dying a little every day ever since it happened. Those who were supposed to love her most didn't care anymore."

Sam came up behind Natalie and put his arms around her.

"I'm glad the funeral is over. I don't think I have much nice to say about that man now," Ruston admitted.

Natalie nodded in agreement. "She still sings like an angel."

"Yes, there wasn't a dry eye in the place." He would have been able to see that when Natalie couldn't.

"Except for her," Natalie said the words. She had noticed too.

"Yes. You see the real Hazel when she sings." He looked at her name on the stone, wishing he had never seen it. Wishing he could forget he ever saw it.

CHAPTER 21

THE TWO WEEKS leading up to the wedding had flown by after the funeral. Hazel had thought it would drag, but it seemed to go by in an instant. Maybe it was because she was actually dreading it. Dreading the wedding, dreading being married, everything.

And it wasn't even that she was not in love with Ruston, she was. Madly, deeply in love with him. But she knew deep down she wasn't right for him. He needed someone better than her, someone who shared his faith.

It wasn't that she had fallen in love with him just in the last few weeks; it was that she had finally allowed herself to love him. She had been falling for him all summer—every time she saw him, talked to him, watched him with her son, she lost a little bit more of her heart until he had it all. Still, she hadn't been able to say the words to him yet.

Last night had been the rehearsal dinner, and she had met Ruston's other brothers and families. It was a lot more people than Hazel had been ready for. Thomas had been there and was making threats to Ruston about things that might be in the ceremony. But she was relaxed—Ruston didn't let it bother him, so she hadn't let it bother her.

She had chosen Natalie, and Ruston had chosen his twin brother to be their witnesses. But they had chosen to stand in front of the church alone together. Neither wanted a big wedding party or a big wedding, just them.

Since Hazel had so few family members, she invited the book club and their significant others to be her family. Having them there had given Hazel familiar faces in the sea of Ruston's family.

Later that night had been her bachelorette party with the book club. Anderson had been kicked out, and the women had taken over Ruth's apartment. They had drunk and talked until the wee hours of the morning and finally went to bed only after Mandy and Mia had fallen asleep on the couch.

She loved her friends and how they had made her feel special all evening. In reality, they hadn't even treated her all that special—it was how they had always treated her. Like she wasn't just one of the triplets or a farmer or a single mother. That she was more than that.

Despite it being late when she had gone to bed in Ruth's spare bedroom with Natalie, she had not been able to sleep. Lying awake, she wondered when the last time she had slept with Natalie had been, but she had been unable to decide when it was. In her mind, she could pinpoint dozens of times, but not the last one. All she knew was that the last time she had slept with her friend, she had not snored. Now she did.

Knowing she would never get any sleep in bed with Natalie anyway, she quietly got up and went to the bathroom. After washing her face, she looked in the mirror. Today was her wedding day. Staring into her hazel eyes, she knew what she had to do today. Sometime. Now.

Leaving the bathroom, she headed for the door, grabbing her coat as she left and shutting the door behind her. Suddenly glad she was in town for the night because the walk would be short. Down the stairs to street level, she headed north and was glad it wasn't so chilly that morning. It could have been freezing by this time in October, but so far, it was still fairly mild out.

Her feet took her quickly down block after block through her hometown. Though she had never walked some of these streets, they were familiar to her. As the church came into view, her steps slowed. Maybe she wasn't ready for this.

Just keep walking, her mind told her as she stepped onto the grass in the cemetery. She had never been this close before, and each step brought her closer until she saw the stone. It was white. And she had seen it from a distance, so she knew which one it was. It didn't matter that she had never seen it up close before. It was the grave she always saw when she was here. The only one she ever saw.

Glancing over, she saw her grandfather's grave with its fresh dirt. She still couldn't feel the pain of losing him. She had lost him years before; it had just taken years to realize it. There was no stone for him yet, but soon.

When she got as close as her legs would carry her to it, she sunk to her knees in the wet grass, not caring that she would be getting her jeans dirty. It didn't matter. "I'm sorry I haven't been here," she whispered into the chilly morning as the sun started to come up. "It's been hard for me."

The sound of a gentle breeze shifting the dry leaves that still clung to the trees was the only sound. Somehow, she expected more from her being there—a sudden storm, or tornado, or even a flood. Not quiet, normal sounds.

"I'm getting married today. I think you guys would like him, but even if you don't, I do. You guys never liked the same things as me anyway." She smiled through her tears. "I wish you were going to be here today. I, we, are standing in front of the church alone, so you two have room to watch. I don't want you to miss it." She pulled a blade of grass and looked at it, needing to focus on something other than the stone with the names and the dates on it. Dates so final.

"I'm friends with Natalie again. We needed to get past your accident. Thank you for being there for her all these years. She needed you too. She's getting married to Mr. Sullivan, and it's as weird as it sounds, but she's so happy. She had to get over you sometime, Henry. You will always be her first love." Her legs were going numb, so she shifted to sit cross-legged. "I don't think it's a surprise she fell for him.

She had it so bad for him senior year. Sorry, Henry, we didn't tell you. But to be fair, you should have seen it also.

"Grandpa is with you guys now. Grandma won't be here long. They changed when you left, and she blamed me for being alive. It made me bitter and sad. It kept me from healing. But I have to, guys. I have to be a better person for Ruston. He deserves so much more than me." She took a breath of chilly air.

"But I'm going to marry him anyway because I am selfish. I want him for me. I've spent so many years not doing anything for me, but today I am going to. Today I am going to marry the man I love, who loves my son and me. Even if he realizes tomorrow what a huge mistake marrying me is, at least I get one day." The tears were dripping from her eyes, forming a pool of water in the folds of her coat.

"I have a son now. He's almost four. I was so excited when I got pregnant, but I wasn't supposed to be. I was in college and in no way ready. He's been my everything since he was born. I don't know if I would have made it without him. I was a mess. But at least they wouldn't have had to order me a gravestone, right?"

She looked at her name in the middle of her siblings' names. Like always, alphabetical. She had sat in the office next to her grandparents as they ordered it, without asking if she wanted her name with theirs. At the time, she had decided that she would be with them soon, so they might as well put her name on it. To her surprise, it was harder to add her last date to it than she had thought it would be.

"I cannot promise that I'll be back. I don't know if I can do this again. But I've put your pictures up in Ruston's house—our house—so I can remember the good times. Because I've dwelt on the bad times for too long, I need to start remembering the good times." Pushing herself to her feet, she looked at their names chiseled in stone. "I love you guys and miss you every day."

Turning, she walked away from them, hoping that she would have the strength to visit again. Time would tell.

CHAPTER 22

Even in his sleep, Ruston knew that Hazel was beside him. He pulled her cold body into his before he was even awake. The fresh air on her cold skin woke him completely.

"What are you doing here, Hazel? We're not supposed to see each other for hours." Or at least that was the plan Natalie had created. Neither of the actual couple had agreed or disagreed with it.

"I needed you now. I needed to be in your arms, just for a little bit. Then I'll go," she whispered.

"I love you." He smiled and kissed the back of her head.

It was something he told her nearly every day. And even if she hadn't said it once, he was sure she felt the same. It was in her actions and the fact that she no longer was against the wedding.

Within moments she was sleeping. Her cold body warmed in his arms as he held her to him. Today she became his forever.

He didn't really believe in the superstition of seeing the bride before the wedding. But he also didn't really want to take chances with Hazel. Then again, here she was, and there was no way he could send her away.

How had she made it past everyone in the house? Thomas was on the couch, and his parents were on a blow-up mattress in John

Henry's room with him. All his brothers and families had driven the two hours home and would make the trip back before the wedding. There were no hotels in Landstad. But they had said it was worth it to see Ruston get married.

Looking down at the woman who was going to be his wife today, he gently touched her cheek. He missed the dimple when it was gone. If he had to put money on it, he would have guessed she would run before she would be in his bed this morning. But she had changed since the first time they had slept together. He wondered if she was more like the Hazel she used to be or if it was a completely new Hazel coming through.

The last two weeks had been surprisingly easy. Since the wedding was small, there had been less stress. Even the funeral hadn't been the landmine of pain for Hazel that Ruston had expected. In fact, the funeral had just made it easier to invite people to the next event.

The book club had been a huge help. Natalie had just gone through all the wedding preparation stuff, so she was priceless in the process. Even Hazel's relationship with Natalie had improved, and they were able to talk and joke together. Just like old times, he assumed.

Pulling away from her, he slid out of bed, grabbed his phone, and went out to the living room. He had to text Natalie to say Hazel was with him because it was better than waking up his bride-to-be. In the living room, he saw why it was so easy for Hazel to get past Thomas— he wasn't there.

He started coffee and sent the text as Thomas snuck in the house carrying a brown bag, which he set on the counter. Handing him a cup of coffee, he asked, "You found someone in less than twelve hours?"

"I can't keep the ladies away, Rusty." Thomas took the coffee from him.

"Did you even try?" Ruston filled another cup.

"I don't kiss and tell." Thomas took a sip of the hot coffee and smiled.

"Yes, you do." Too much information sometimes, way too much.

"You got a nice little town here. I was looking for my own Hazel."

"Did you find her?"

"We'll see what I can make of it."

"Good luck."

"So here we are. You're marrying that crazy good singer you met, well, you know, at a party. I'm not surprised you had it bad the night of the party. If you had been able to find her, you would have married her that day." Thomas sat down on the couch with his coffee. He seemed well-rested after his night out.

"I knew where to find her already. But if I knew she would've agreed, I would have," he confirmed with a grin.

"Any doubts?" Thomas's eyebrow went up in question.

"Not really. I worry that she's only marrying me because I kind of forced her."

"If she didn't want to marry you, she wouldn't be marrying you." Thomas's words mirrored the ones he had been trying to believe for weeks.

Hazel can be bullied, but not into something she doesn't want.

"She worries about being my wife. Or actually just the wife of a preacher," he told Thomas, something that he hadn't told anyone. Even his dad.

"Are you going to force your religion down her throat?" Thomas asked.

"Of course not, it's up to her. It would be nice for her to attend my services and be a part of the church." He'd had a vision of what his wife would be, but he didn't know if Hazel would conform to that vision. Or even if that vision was a reality for any woman.

"Does she?" Thomas looked into the cup he was holding with a questioning expression on his face.

"Not since her grandfather went into the hospital." Ruston rolled his eyes at his friend.

"Have you asked her to?" Thomas handed him the empty cup.

"Every week." Getting up, he refilled his friend's cup.

"Have you asked her to go for you? Not for her?" Thomas smiled at the full cup.

"I don't want her to go just because *I* want her to go. I want her to go because she wants to go." He had thought about it many times over the weeks they had been together, and the ones when he had wanted them together. He had no real answers.

"Maybe she has to go for you for a while, and that will turn into her going for her. Maybe that first step is going to be the hard one, the one she needs help with," Thomas suggested.

"I never thought of it that way," Ruston said.

"That's why I'm better at this than you. And I am on the outside looking in. You're right in the middle of it."

Ruston looked at his best friend and knew he was right. He was too close to see it. He wanted Hazel to instantly realize that God did love her and that she loved him, but it was going to take time, days, months—maybe years. He had to be there to help her along the way, sometimes beside her and sometimes leading or pushing.

Suddenly a weight was lifted off his heart at Hazel's lack of love for his God. It would come with time. She had been there once. She would come back in her own time.

The door to his bedroom opened, and Hazel hesitated as she came out of the room. Her eyes locked with Thomas's, and she blushed at being caught in his bedroom.

"You know, Rusty, you were supposed to spend one last night alone." Thomas slapped him on the back, but it was more of a giggle than a laugh.

"I wasn't here all night, just an hour or so," Hazel said as she climbed into Ruston's lap. If she was trying to disprove that they hadn't spent the night together, her actions were not helping.

She was warm in his arms, not the freezing cold of earlier in the morning. He hadn't asked why she was there earlier, and he wasn't going to ask now. That she wanted to be with him was the most important part.

"Doesn't matter to me. I just like to see Rusty happy. And you've been making him happy since summer."

"How much do you really know, Thomas?" Hazel asked but didn't lift her head from his chest.

"I know enough, Hazel May. I know that you lost your shoes, and he lost his heart at a house party. I knew I would be right here one day, marrying you two, because my buddy was done for."

"I hope you don't say that in Ruston's church. They jumped to the wrong conclusions when my car was parked at his place too long." Hazel's words reminded him of why she might actually be marrying him: to save his good name.

"I will keep it close and blackmail you two when I need to," Thomas promised.

"Good. We'll gladly be blackmailed by you." Ruston held her tighter in his arms.

"So, Hazel, are you mad at Rusty for forcing your hand? You could have said no," Thomas asked, ignoring Ruston's glares.

Hazel stiffened in his arms, and he wanted to kill his best friend. Why was he reminding Hazel that she could have said no, could still say no? That until the actual wedding, she could walk away.

But she said, "No, I understand why he had to marry me. I just hope he doesn't regret it."

"Will you regret it?" Thomas asked her.

"No. Even if he leaves me tomorrow, at least I had one day of happiness with him," she whispered in his arms.

He didn't even know if Thomas heard her, but Ruston did, and he kissed the top of her head, his heart soaring at her words. "I will never leave you, Haze," he whispered back.

With a text from Natalie to send to Hazel, he reluctantly let her walk back the four blocks to downtown. Watching her walk away, he knew Thomas had been right, but he might have started to fall for her every Sunday as she sat with her son, just watching him.

CHAPTER 23

"Are you supposed to not be able to breathe in your wedding dress?" Hazel asked the group of her friends in the basement of the church.

"Of course, you're not," Tess said from a chair.

"That's what makes your wedding day so memorable, the constant panic of passing out," Mia said and moved a lock of hair on Hazel's head.

"Did you at least bring a paper bag for me?" Hazel asked her personal attendant. Or everyone's personal attendant since Mia was nearly a professional at this.

"Of course," Mia said. "I put the professional in charge of it."

Nurse practitioner Mandy Nordskov pulled out the bag from her purse and showed it to the room. Hazel was sure the woman had more than a paper bag with her. She was most likely ready for any medical emergency she came across.

Hazel was fully dressed in the tight white dress and white tennis shoes since heels were not her thing. Her hair was professionally done, even if she didn't think two-inch-long hair needed a professional. Mia had insisted. Instead of a veil, the hairdresser had added a halo of tiny white flowers on her head. It had looked breathtaking when Hazel had finally looked at herself in a mirror. She didn't even have to wonder if Ruston would like it; she knew he would.

Ruston's parents had taken charge of John Henry for the day, so Hazel had nothing to worry about with her son. Not that she had to worry about him—the entire book club would make sure he was the center of attention.

"Don't bite your lips, Haze. You don't want me to reapply the lipstick." Natalie held up the tube as she said it.

Sticking her tongue out at her friend, she stopped the nervous habit. She did not want to have to get it reapplied before the ceremony. She hated makeup and would not have any on if it hadn't been for Natalie. Well, she hated girly makeup, though, given the chance, she would put on some punk rock makeup. They were not the same thing.

"You guys can go sit down. It's almost time," she said to her friends. She needed a moment alone to think.

"Are you going to run?" Mia asked the question Hazel knew was going through everyone's mind.

"I will not pull a Natalie." Hazel smirked and looked at her oldest friend, who stuck her tongue out at her.

"If you do, Haze, the keys are in my Jeep." Mia gave her a hug. It was the same line she gave Natalie a few months before. Natalie had taken the out, but Hazel couldn't imagine leaving Ruston behind. It would be like leaving a piece of herself behind.

"I don't need them, but thanks," she whispered.

Then she hugged each one as they left to get up to sit by their significant others since she was the first in their group to get married. Natalie would be next, as Sam had asked her in a very public way. Watching them go, she loved that they were her friends, even though a year before, she would never have thought it possible that any of them would be close.

Closing her eyes, she tried to relax. Just breathe. Someone would tell her when it was time to go. Spinning her engagement ring on her finger, she relaxed.

"You look beautiful, Hazel." Her grandma's voice made her open her eyes.

"Thank you, I feel beautiful," she admitted.

She had invited the woman but had been sure she wouldn't come. It had been weeks since they had talked, and that hadn't gone well.

"Nice weather for a wedding," her grandmother said. Always the weather.

"It'll do. I would marry him in any weather." She smiled because it was true. Rain couldn't dampen this day.

"So, you love him?"

"Yes, I do, and he's good with John Henry. He's good for me."

"I am happy for you," the woman said, but she didn't seem happy. In fact, she seemed like she was anything but happy.

"I'm happy for me too." Hazel ignored her mood and asked the one question she needed an answer to. "Did you stop loving me after the accident?"

"Of course not." She took a step away from her granddaughter as she answered.

"It felt like you did, both of you." Hazel didn't move, didn't dare.

"We did no such thing," she argued.

"Did you want me dead too?" She asked, knowing she didn't really want an answer, but she needed to know before she walked down the aisle to her new life. One final answer.

"It would have been easier, Hazel. You have no idea how hard it was to look at you. You were the same as Hanna."

"It was hard for you? I lost my best friends. All of them. And I lost my grandparents all in one day. I was lost for years. I almost didn't survive it." Had her grandma seen how destructive she had been, or hadn't she even cared at that point?

"You were a constant reminder that they were gone." Her grandmother's words hurt her.

"Don't you think I saw that? I see her face every day. But you know what? It's my face too. I've had to learn to live without them. I didn't for years; I just let the pain consume me. I'm finally letting go of that pain because I can't live with it anymore. I don't want pain to be the only thing I feel." Hazel forced herself not to cry, not moments before she got married.

"I'm glad that you can do that, Hazel," her grandmother said bitterly.

"Do you love me anymore?" Hazel asked again, not letting the woman go without answering the question.

"No, I had to let go of that when I lost them. I couldn't handle losing you too, so I let you all go when I put them in the ground," her grandmother admitted.

"Did you at least love my son?" she demanded of the woman who spent as much time with him as she had since his birth.

"He's busy," was all she said.

"Do you even want to be here? Watching me, *Hazel*, get married? Watching me, *Hazel*, be happy?" She emphasized her name each time she said it, making sure the other woman knew who she was talking to. Not a ghost of her sister.

"I've not been looking forward to the day."

"You don't have to be here then."

"Are you throwing me out of your wedding?" The woman actually acted like Hazel had done something wrong, not her.

"No, I am saying that if you don't want to be here, don't be. I have a church full of people who love me. Really love me. And they have been looking forward to this day. They want to be here. Because I didn't die six years ago, and I am tired of being treated like I should have," Hazel said as she saw Ruston in the doorway.

Not Ruston, of course. It was Randy. She could tell them apart, but at first glance, she would always see Ruston, her husband. Without giving the older woman a hug, she said, "I have to go get married now. Do what you want."

Lifting her dress, she walked away from her grandmother and toward her future. It was up to her grandmother to be a part of that future. All Hazel knew was that she was not going to let the pain of loss make her bitter and unable to love those still alive. A weight had been lifted off her chest about the guilt and pain she had felt for six years about what she could not change.

Randy left her with his wife and another of Ruston's brothers' wives to fix her gown just outside the closed doors of the sanctuary. As the woman straightened and smoothed her dress, she looked over her shoulder at her grandma standing a few feet from her. Hazel smiled at the older woman, but she didn't smile back, she just turned and walked away from her. Forever.

Turning to Ashley, she whispered something to her as the doors opened to the church full of people. But all she saw was Ruston standing at the end of the aisle in the front of the church. With a deep breath and a smile, she started walking slowly toward her future.

CHAPTER 24

EVERY TIME RUSTON SAW HAZEL, she took his breath away. She had been sexy singing on that stage at the house party, and she had been pretty sitting in church with her son on her lap. She was adorable when she slept peacefully beside him, she was lovely even when she cried, and she was delightful when she laughed. But she was stunning on her wedding day. He wanted to run to her as she walked down the aisle toward him. It took Thomas putting a hand on his sleeve to keep him in place. Her hair was in an amazing style that had flowers woven into it. Her dimple was there in her smile.

He wanted to kiss that dimple.

Every few steps, he saw a white tennis shoe poke out from under her dress, making him think of her boots still in his office. Maybe tomorrow he would give them back; tomorrow she would be his.

When she was close enough, he reached out his hand, and she took it, locking her hazel eyes onto his as she took the last few steps to him. She stopped and turned to him as if she did it every day, like they had practiced the night before.

Leaning in, he kissed her dimple and said, "You look stunning."

She whispered, "I love you too."

Pulling back, he looked into her eyes, and she bit her lip and started to blush at her words. Instantly, he knew she had thought he had said the words, and she had mirrored them, but did she mean them? Before he could say anything, Thomas started the ceremony.

Ruston had officiated dozens of weddings and knew the words by heart, but he wasn't listening to them now. All he could do was look at the beautiful woman in front of him and dream of their future.

Glancing out at their friends and family in the pews, he saw his mom and dad and his brothers and families. There was the book club and their boyfriends or friends. John Henry was now sitting with Natalie, who was crying with Sam's arm around her. Hazel's grandmother was no longer in the seat she was in earlier. He didn't know what to think about that.

Eyes back on his bride, he reached up and ran a finger down her jawline. The action made Hazel hold back a laugh and she mouthed "Stop" at him. But he just needed to touch her. She took his hand back in hers with a smile.

Thomas was still talking about something, so he tried to concentrate on what he was going on about. They had practiced last night, and he knew what was happening, but he was surprised when Thomas actually went and sat in the spot where her grandmother was supposed to be.

Turning to Hazel, he saw she was looking at her feet. Was she going to leave? He should have paid more attention to the ceremony. He had just wanted it over so he could kiss her.

Her eyes slowly raised until they were looking into his, and she started to sing—no instruments, just Hazel. To his delight, she started with the first three lines of "Life in a Northern Town," from the house party. She sang it so quietly that he wondered if anyone in the church could even hear her, but he did. And maybe that was why she was singing so quietly.

As those lines stopped, she started to loudly sing the entire song of "I Can't Help Falling in Love with You," making him want to cry. And maybe he did. He didn't think he was the only one. Just as she finished, John Henry broke away from Natalie and rushed to his mom. Ruston caught the little boy in his little black suit and lifted him into his arms, settling him on his hip as he pulled her to him and kissed her on the lips. Her arms went around him, and she sighed as he deepened the kiss.

Remembering that they had an audience, he pulled away, and she bit her lip and blushed. With cheers from the audience to do it again, he did, but just a light kiss this time.

Thomas came back up and walked between them, breaking their contact. "Stop it. I am almost done," he said to the couple, who were now three standing before him.

Without a thought, Thomas took John Henry out of Ruston's arms and said, "We can't do the vows with you holding him. I will hold him; you hold her hands."

And with that, Thomas led them through their vows and the exchanging of the rings. Once that was all done, she was his wife, ring and all. Thomas handed the boy back to Ruston and announced, "I'd like to introduce Mr. and Mrs. Abbott and family of Landstad, North Dakota."

CHAPTER 25

A WEEK after she and Ruston exchanged vows, Hazel had the house she had always called home completely empty. The house had been the same for as long as she could remember until now. Now it was ready for another family. Hazel didn't know who would buy it and didn't want to. It was no longer home to her.

Home was now wherever Ruston was. Ruston and John Henry. Hazel had thought it would take time to get used to living in another house, but it hadn't. The transition had been seamless. Not even John Henry had questioned the move from the farm. His excitement over having his own room had made her feel guilty for always keeping him so close to her.

So far, she hadn't even spoken to her grandma, though the older woman had been through the house and took some stuff while Hazel had been gone one day. Most had been left for her granddaughter to deal with. Nearly everything had been sold or thrown out. There wasn't much in the house that had been worth even taking to town, but Ruston had a completely furnished house, so they didn't need the things anyway. Hazel didn't need the memories the things would bring either.

Hazel had started her married life with nothing from her past but a few photos and her son. Even after only a week, she could tell it had been the right move, one she should have done long ago. Without the constant feeling that nothing had happened, and everything was as if they were coming home, Hazel was able to look at her siblings' smiling faces and think of the good times instead.

Rolling over in bed, she missed her husband. He had gotten up first, and she could hear him in the shower getting ready for his day. Debating whether she should join him or not, her decision was made when John Henry walked into the room carrying his stuffed monkey.

With the move into the house, John henry had been upgrade to his own bed. No longer was he trapped until someone took him out. So, he was free to get out of bed and wander through the house. For the first time in his life, he was able to just crawl into his mom's bed unannounced. Sometimes it was a good surprise, and sometimes a bad one.

"Morning, baby," she said to him as he climbed into the bed.

"Morning, Mommy." He looked toward the door he knew Ruston was behind.

"Ruston's in the shower," Hazel told him, and he just nodded.

"Ruston was hoping for company, but I can see you already have some." He stood in the open doorway, wearing just a towel around his hips.

"I was thinking about it, then not." She looked him over from his wet hair to his bare feet.

"Ruston," John Henry said and scurried off the bed to go to him. No doubt the boy loved to spend time with the new man in his life.

"Morning, John Henry." He lifted the boy into his arms. Hazel secretly hoped the towel would fall, but it held. "Morning, wife."

"Husband." She grinned and fell back onto the pillow, letting him deal with the little boy.

"What are you doing today?" Ruston sat on the bed next to her, John Henry on his lap.

"I don't know. The house is cleaned out now." She looked at the ceiling that had occupied her days all week.

"Come to church." He ran a finger over her shoulder.

"Why?" She turned and looked at him.

"Because it's Sunday, and I want you there." His finger continued its trail down her arm.

Groaning, she looked up at him. "Are you sure it's Sunday?"

"Positive." He lifted her hand and kissed the back of it as John Henry jumped from his lap and left the room.

"Won't you be nervous with me watching you work?" she teased.

"Please, Haze?" he asked as he set her hand down.

From the day she had said yes to marrying him, she knew this day was coming. He wanted her to go to church. There was no getting away from it; when she put his ring on, she had agreed to it. Not that that knowledge had made her any more willing to go. He hadn't asked her before they got married, and she was hoping he wouldn't push after.

"For me." His sad blue eyes bore into her.

Rolling away from him, she mumbled into her pillow, "Fine."

His hand slid down her bare back, and he kissed it as he said, "Thank you, Hazel May."

* * *

THREE HOURS LATER, Hazel was sitting beside Natalie, wishing she had just said no to that man. He was all smiles in front of the sanctuary, but she was not. Natalie was more fidgety than John Henry and kept leaning to Sam or Hazel to say something.

Looking across to where she used to sit, the pew was empty. When she had first arrived, she had wondered how she was going to not sit with her grandma, but the older woman had not shown up. Natalie had said she hadn't been there the day after the wedding either. Hazel did not know what that meant. Was she never coming back to church because Hazel was married to the minister now? Or was it because she was there, period?

Had the older woman finally found a way for her to not have Hazel in her life? Could she now move on with her life without the reminder of the grandkids she lost? Had Hazel been that easy to leave?

"He keeps looking at you, Hazel. You have to pretend to want to be here," Natalie whispered to her as Ruston delivered his sermon.

"Quit talking, Natalie," she whispered back without looking at her friend.

"I mean, you don't have to go all-in, just a little singing or something. Just fake it," Natalie said, as if Hazel hadn't told her to not talk.

"Quit talking," Hazel said again.

"Do you like his hair curly or straight? I mean, he looks handsome with it all combed, but when it curls, you know," Natalie continued, even though her boyfriend was just on the other side of her.

"Natalie, we are in church," Hazel hissed.

"Just saying, Haze …" Her words dropped off as Sam slid his arm around her and covered her mouth with his hand. The move made Natalie turn her attention to the man on the other side of her.

Looking up at her husband, Hazel decided she liked his hair curly better. She hadn't told him yet, but he might already know. Today she might have listened to the sermon, but Natalie had talked the entire time. Or maybe she wouldn't have, because she hadn't in years. As he talked, he noticed her looking at him and smiled. She was unable not to smile back at him.

Closing his bible, he announced a song was going to be sung, and the organist started the play the familiar tune. But today, she was unable to sing the words out loud that were playing in her head. Even for Ruston.

So far, she could sit here for him, but being a part of it was going to take time. If it ever happened at all.

CHAPTER 26

LATER IN THE WEEK, plans had changed from an evening at home alone to a trip down to Grand Forks to see Tess and Math's new baby. Ruston had talked Hazel into them driving separate from the rest of the book club so he could spend some time with Thomas. The guys would grab a meal while the ladies looked at the baby.

At the last moment, Natalie and Sam joined them. It seemed Natalie could still push Hazel around, and sometimes it was a good thing. Natalie and Sam made the car ride jovial.

So at 6:00 p.m., Hazel dropped off Ruston, John Henry, and Sam for their man's night. Thomas took them to a popular restaurant in town. The place was busy and maybe too loud for a little boy, but he seemed to be doing okay and happy to be with Ruston.

Even though the men had seen each other less than two weeks before, they had a lot of catching up to do. After rehashing the wedding for a few minutes, Ruston asked, "Did you ever call that woman from the dance?"

Thomas looked confused. "No."

"You should. You'll like her. Everyone likes her," Ruston said of Mia. She was what Thomas needed in his life. They had similar personalities, and both were extremely outgoing.

"I don't remember her," Thomas admitted with a frown.

"Brunette, shorter," Sam replied, knowing who Ruston was talking about right away.

"Nope." He shook his head in confession at them both.

"Still hung up on Kit then?" Ruston laughed, knowing what was really happening. The man had admitted who he had spent the night with, and Ruston had broken it to him that she was not exactly who he was looking for. Except suddenly, his best friend wasn't looking for a woman who was his type anymore but at the blonde former resident of Landstad.

"No, she's just a coworker," he said firmly.

"Wait! You work with her? You never said anything about that." Ruston laughed at his friend. He had it bad. It would be sweet revenge if Ruston wasn't so happy for the man.

"You never asked," Thomas said with a shrug.

"I've always gotten along with her. She's nice. Have you been seeing her?" Sam asked, joining in the conversation.

"Just at work. Because we work together," Thomas reminded him.

"How about the kids thing? And she's older than you," Ruston pointed out.

"We're not dating, we just talk. At work. We're work friends." Thomas was not admitting to anything, but Ruston knew him well enough to see that his friend was very into the blonde. And it was rare that Thomas spent more than a week with one woman, in his bed or even on his mind. Kit seemed to have been different in more ways than the obvious.

"Okay, I'll drop it. For now. Can I tell Hazel yet?" Ruston asked, hating that he hadn't told her that Thomas had hooked up with a local. Not that Hazel would care, but she would spread the word to her friend, who was related to Kit.

"There's nothing to tell."

"So you keep saying."

"I will definitely not tell Natalie, or the entire town will know. I know my woman well." Sam chuckled at his own outgoing fiancé.

Their meals came, and the men and the boy dug into the food

before them, their conversation stopping almost completely. Ruston helped his new son eat—John Henry became distracted easily, and Ruston got him back on task.

"What do you know about the accident?" Thomas asked from out of nowhere.

"What accident?" Ruston stopped eating, wondering if the man could actually be talking about the only accident Ruston thought about.

"Hazel's. Or not Hazel's, actually," Thomas replied, setting down his fork.

It was exactly how Ruston thought of it. Hazel's accident. Even if the woman hadn't been in the accident, she had been so close to it. She had lost so much in it.

"Not a lot, but enough. I know more about the fallout after than the actual accident itself. It messed her up pretty good for a long time. Messed up a lot of people. Why?" Ruston put down his silverware.

"Kit's brother-in-law was in the accident," he said.

"I guess she is a Smith, and he was a Smith. I never made the connection before. I wonder if Hazel remembers. I don't think she would have let Kit watch John Henry for the wedding if she had. She distances herself from everyone in the accident." Ruston leaned back in the booth. It made sense that there was another family affected by the accident. The third victim was from town as well. His family should be around somewhere. But Kit Nordskov was a surprise. He wondered if Hazel knew or remembered.

"Everyone involved does, guys. I was there that night as part of the volunteer fire department then. I saw it. I try not to think about it, but I understand where you both are coming from on this. Natalie has the scars that show, and others do not." Sam leaned into the table.

"I think Kit has those inner scars as well," Thomas remarked as a text from Hazel came that she was on her way to pick them up.

After the bills were paid, everyone got their jackets on, including John Henry, who insisted he could do it himself until the moment he couldn't. Then he needed Ruston to do it for him.

After waving goodbye to Thomas, Ruston got the boy into his car seat, and the other couple climbed in the back of the car. Ruston got in beside Hazel. In the week since they got married, she had started to drive his SUV most of the time, mostly because he hated her driving the little car since the weather could turn to snow at any moment. So far, she hadn't said anything about not driving her little yellow bug around. Soon they would have to think about getting her own newer car.

"How was the baby?" he asked as he shut the door.

"Cute. Tess is a natural mom." She put the car into gear.

"Just like you are, Haze," Natalie said from the back seat

"No, very different from me. I had no experience with kids when I had John Henry. I just had to figure it out."

"Didn't your grandma help?" he asked, then regretted it. So far, the two hadn't spoken since the wedding. Something happened, and she wasn't ready to talk about it yet.

"No, I was still in college when he was born, so I was away. She wasn't happy I had him. They both thought they would have to raise him, so they didn't help, probably in hopes I would give him up for adoption," she answered as she drove.

"Like you three?" he said quietly. The entire car knew who the older couple had to raise.

"Yes, Grandma admitted she regretted taking us in. That she should have let my mom put us up for adoption when we were babies." Her words took him by surprise. The woman had actually told her grandchild that? But she had told a near-stranger, so why not her granddaughter?

"When did she tell you?" He was learning the woman didn't try to protect the kids' feelings.

"Many times when we were growing up. Three was too much for them. They were old." Hazel repeated the excuse her grandmother had said, but the couple wasn't all that old twenty years ago. The older couple were not as old as they let on. They had to be close to forty when they had taken in the three children.

"Maybe they shouldn't have said that out loud," Ruston stated and heard agreement from the back seat. Though the other couple was not participating in the conversation, they were listening.

"They were very good grandparents until the accident. Then they changed. From that night on, they were not the same people who raised us," Hazel said into the dark windshield.

"Why didn't your grandma come to the wedding, Hazel?" He hadn't asked before. It was between the two of them, but today he wanted to know no matter who was in the car.

"She couldn't be happy for me, so I told her not to stay." She shrugged.

"Is it me?" he asked. Though he had known the couple for years, maybe they thought he wasn't good enough for her granddaughter.

"No, it has always been me. Me being alive still," she said so matter-of-factly that he had to look at her in the dark car.

"How can she blame you for surviving an accident you weren't even in? I can see her being angry that Natalie survived, but you weren't even in the car that night." He had forgotten for a moment Natalie was actually in the car with them, but she didn't say anything from the back seat.

"We were three, a set. We should have been together. I should have been there."

"Hazel, you can't blame yourself for surviving," Natalie finally stated.

"I didn't say I blame myself," Hazel argued with her friend, but everyone in the car knew she was lying.

"You didn't have to. You lived with them blaming you for six years, and it made you miserable," Ruston said before Natalie could say anything.

"Can we not talk about this?" Hazel said, her voice low.

Was it because she didn't want to talk about it at all or because the other couple was in the car? He was willing to bet that it was the former. Talking out the situation was hard for her.

"Okay," he agreed reluctantly, not wanting to make her mad at him. "But I do have to tell you that Thomas is falling for Kit Nordskov."

"Mandy's sister?" Hazel questioned with interest.

"Yes, but she was also Jamie Smith's sister-in-law. I don't know if you remembered that."

Hearing her gasp in the dark car said that she hadn't. Either she hadn't known or hadn't remembered. The two were years apart in age and didn't run in the same circles until recently. Now she was friends with both Kit's brother and sister.

"They met at the wedding, or actually, they work together and hooked up at the wedding. I think she would be really good for him, but I wanted you to know." He knew he couldn't keep it from her. She needed to know.

"I don't remember her at the wedding," Hazel said.

"She was at the wedding but not the reception," Sam said from the back seat.

"She left early, but they hooked up the night before." Ruston wondered if he had said too much. Natalie was known for running her mouth, and she was definitely listening. "But this needs to not go anywhere. I don't think Kit wants her parents to know yet."

"So, no telling anyone," Sam said flatly, more to Natalie than Hazel.

"You know I would never tell anyone," Natalie said with a huff. Even she knew she would have trouble keeping her mouth shut.

The car fell silent, with only Sam and Natalie talking quietly to each other, probably because John Henry was sleeping in his car seat between them. Hazel was completely silent as she drove through the night. Ruston left her alone. She needed time to think about Kit being friends with Thomas. Or maybe she wasn't thinking about it at all. He had no idea. Maybe her mind was on nothing but the accident and Kit's connection to it.

CHAPTER 27

THURSDAY. The anniversary of the accident fell on a Thursday that year. Hazel had not been looking forward to it, just like every other year. Ruston hadn't seemed to remember that it was today, if he even knew.

Trying to keep her mind off the events of the day, she cleaned the nearly spotless house. Scrubbing the floors, then walls when she ran out of floors. Then she vacuumed all the carpets and furniture. By lunchtime, she was rearranging the kitchen cabinets, though she just seemed to be putting everything back where it had been before. She hadn't really wanted to change things in Ruston's house, not wanting to mess up any part of his life.

Ruston took John Henry back with him to the church for the afternoon to get him out of her hair. With all the cleaning, he was getting on her nerves when he would mess up something. It was best if he was out of the house.

Her goal for the day had been not to cry at all. So far, she had succeeded in her effort, but just barely. Today she had avoided looking at the pictures she had so recently put on the walls, of the smiling happy teens forever trapped in time.

At one point, she thought Natalie would come over, but she knew her friend was in her own private hell today. Same as she was. Some days were not worth sharing.

At three in the afternoon, a light snow had started to fall, so unlike the day seven years before when it had been bright, sunny, and warm all day. With nothing else to do, she walked across the street to get John Henry, so she wouldn't be alone. Loneliness was setting in as the day progressed.

She found the boy sleeping in Ruston's office, with her husband working at his desk. He smiled at her, and she just waved, leaving the boy to sleep as long as he needed to. No need for a crabby boy and a crabby mom.

Instead of turning to leave the church and go back across the snowy street, she walked into the sanctuary. It was dark and quiet, so different from Sunday mornings with its brightness and people milling around.

Lightly touching the smooth wood of the pews as she walked past them, she went toward the front of the church. In her heart, she knew that was when you prayed, but she wasn't there yet.

Looking around the room, her eyes landed on the old piano she had learned to play on. When the triplets were six, their grandmother had dutifully brought them every week to learn to play little songs with Mrs. Green, who was long since gone. Of the three, only Hazel loved it. The other two were no longer playing by seven. But Hazel came back, year after year, even when her grandmother didn't want to bring her anymore. When Mrs. Green wasn't able to teach her anything more, she was just there as Hazel played.

At one point, she had begged her grandparents for a piano, but they had always said no, only getting her a guitar when she had changed to begging for that. Neither had ever understood her love of music and had barely tolerated it when she was young. And when she came back, they didn't. Even the radio was silent most days in the house unless she was alone.

Sitting down at the old familiar instrument, she opened the lid silently, then ran her fingers lightly over the keys, pressing them just enough for them not to make a sound. There was still a chip on the middle C key, and she ran a finger over it, a finger that remembered it even when Hazel didn't.

Lightly, she played the songs that Mrs. Green had taught her so many years before. Using only three fingers, then four, then finally five. Then adding the other hand to it. Looking at the music in front of her on the stand, she started playing. She knew it was the last song sung on Sunday morning, but it wasn't one she had ever played before. But the notes played as easy as any song.

Turning the page, she played the next song, then the next. Lost in playing, she started to hum the tune as she played. After an entire day of trying to not think about the day seven years before, she was finally able to relax. To not think about what today was.

During the fourth song, a sleepy John Henry climbed onto the bench beside her. As she continued to play, he would poke a random key, and she would play over it. As he did it once, then twice, he got bolder and started to play with two hands himself.

Instantly she stopped playing and pulled him onto her lap. Putting his hands in the proper position on the keyboard, she showed him the basics, playing a few notes and humming as she did it.

With a wiggly body, he followed her lead and played the keys she played and hummed. Not the same melody she was playing, but it didn't matter. Today she needed to share this part of her life with him, a part that had made her special, apart from being one of three.

"He's going to be as good as his mom," Ruston said from behind her.

She hadn't even noticed he had followed her son into the room. "He'll be better than me. I'm not overly good." She let John Henry play the song as best he could, which wasn't good, so she showed him again.

"So you say, but I know better. You're an amazing musician, no matter what you play or sing." Ruston rested his hands on her shoulders.

"I just like to play," she whispered as his thumbs rubbed the back of her neck.

"You have a gift, Hazel. Don't let anyone tell you differently. An amazing gift that you should be sharing." His hands relaxed muscles she didn't even know were tense.

"You can't make money from music, Ruston." She watched as John Henry poked at the keys again. He might be too young to learn to play.

"Yes, you can. You can teach it, and you can play it." He kissed the top of her head. "Do you want me to take him so you can relax?"

"No, I can take care of him." She started to slide off the bench. Her son was far more important than music was.

"So can I. You need some alone time today. Here's as good of a place as any." His hands stopped her movements, and he took the boy off her lap. "Come home when you're ready."

"I will," she said, trying not to cry, because she wasn't going to today. But he was making it hard when he was being so good to her. When she didn't deserve it.

Unable to move, she heard the front door shut as Ruston left her alone. But still, she wasn't able to play again. Memories were her enemy today, and now they were winning. Memories of her siblings talking about their futures, colleges, and jobs. Things she had never dreamed of. When she had decided on a college, it was for their music program, even if there would be no jobs for her when she graduated from it. Her dream had been unachievable compared to theirs.

Henry was going to farm, and Hanna was going to be a teacher. They had their plans set. By now they would both be done with school and living their lives. Would they be married yet? Have kids? If they had lived, would she have had John Henry? Would she be there? Would she have come home to visit and met Ruston the normal way, not having him forced to marry her?

"I broke up with Henry that night. That's why he was speeding. He was mad at me. So mad he wasn't being careful. And we were all too drunk to care." Natalie's voice broke her questions.

That Natalie was there hadn't surprised her. She had been so much a part of Hazel's life that not having her there would have surprised her. Even in this most private time, Natalie was a part of it. She was the only person who understood.

Silently, Hazel closed the lid of the piano. She would not play again today. But it was here when she needed it, and she would need it again eventually.

"I should have told you. I don't know when I would have, but I want you to know. I broke his heart. Before he died, I broke his heart." She was standing, staring out a stained-glass window, not even looking at Hazel.

"Why?" Hazel asked, looking at her friend across the dark sanctuary, knowing her friend was in as much pain today her she was.

"I didn't want to have sex with him," she admitted, with Jesus looking down at her from that window. Instantly she blushed and turned, looking over at Hazel.

"I mean, why are you telling me now?" Hazel asked.

"You should know. I had stopped being a good friend to Hanna for Henry, and then I dumped him, and then they both died. First you, then Hanna, then Henry. I let every one of you down, and then I lived." Natalie's voice was breaking over the sobs as she spoke.

"It's not our fault. It was an accident."

"I know, we were stupid kids. We thought we had the rest of our lives, and that nothing could touch us. I want that day back so badly."

"We can't have any day back, Natalie."

"I'm sorry, Hazel May." Natalie sat down in the pew closest to the piano Hazel was still sitting at. She hadn't been able to move.

"Why?"

"Because I was an awful person to you for years. I spent today watching movies." Natalie's dad had made movies of all her life's events, big and small. All ball games, dances, even just playing in the back yard. Hanna and Hazel had been caught in those videos time and again. Hazel hadn't seen many but knew they existed.

"You shouldn't. Not today." Hazel had no idea when a good day would be, but not then, when everything was so raw.

"Today is the best day for it. I'm already crying, so I spent the entire day watching. I had forgotten about so much." She drew up her knees, rested her chin on them.

"Like what?"

"You being there. I always remember Hanna there, but you were there too, in the background. I wish you were in the front."

"That's not me. I am background."

"I saw Jamie in some of the videos, the later ones. He really liked Hanna. I didn't remember that. I always felt it was a short little relationship. Something that happened suddenly and wouldn't last." She sniffed and wiped away her tears. "That Henry and I were so much better of a couple."

"They had been together for most of the summer," Hazel remembered. He had come to get her for dates for months. Hazel didn't go anywhere, she remembered.

"I thought it started that fall. But the movies tell the real story. I wish I could talk to her about him, ask her what she felt for him. Did she tell you?"

"No, but we weren't close then," Hazel said, knowing that Natalie already knew that.

"Nor were we," Natalie admitted, and Hazel knew she meant her and Hanna.

"I don't think about him. Ever." He was the third that died that day. In her place, she always felt. But she never thought about him as a person to be missed. A person who was missed.

"Me neither. At least Kit does." Natalie sniffed again. "At least someone does."

CHAPTER 28

"WELCOME, KIT," Ruston said to Thomas's lady love. Thomas had just spent two days arranging for this covert meal, so he could see her during the four-day Thanksgiving break she was spending with her parents. Convenient that they were in the same town as his best friend.

Since the couple had been together for a short time, and Kit was in no way telling her parents about the relationship, everything was on the down-low. There were even cover stories for the couple as to where they were supposed to be. One was to be out with her sister and one … Well, it didn't matter, he wasn't hiding anything.

"Thank you for inviting me. I only brought the little two. I thought John Henry would like to have a friend. You invited the right person to have a playmate for him." Kit took the toddler from Thomas's arms and took off his little jacket.

Kit had five boys, three from her first marriage, who were around ten, and two from her second, who were John Henry's age and younger. When Thomas had first come up with this night, Ruston wasn't sure he was ready for five kids and two more adults in his house.

At the first sign she was there, Thomas had rushed out to meet her at the car to help with her two younger kids. Just that alone made Ruston know his friend was completely smitten with this woman. Thomas had been completely against the idea of stepkids his entire life. But not anymore, it seemed. Not with this woman.

Now Ruston knew his buddy was in love for sure, and that was even before Ruston saw that his friend was unable to take his eyes off the woman. Not that she wasn't doing her share of quick glances at Thomas either, which meant this might turn into something that lasted forever for his friend.

"That's not why you were invited, Kit. It was all Thomas's doing," Hazel said from the kitchen doorway, not quite part of the group. She was acting distant from the woman who was also thinking about the accident. Their only connection being the biggest tragedy of their lives.

"It did have the stink of him on it." Kit laughed, her eyes not leaving Thomas's, who just rolled hearsays at her joke.

"I have no stink." Thomas helped her remove her jacket.

Ruston didn't miss the small ways he touched her as he did it.

"Hi, Hazel," Kit said as she put Josiah down. Though the boys had seen each other at church, they were still virtual strangers. But they were keeping the other in eyesight.

"Hi, Kit," Hazel replied, not moving from her spot, still away from the group, not joining.

Ruston had removed James from his seat and held on to him. His eye caught Hazel's, and he wondered if she was thinking about the kids they would have as well. Or were her thoughts trapped in the past with Kit there? The future too hard to think about when the past was so present.

"I can take James," Thomas said, reaching for the baby. Ruston watched Hazel's eyes go to the baby wearily. She must not have known the baby's name was James … after Jamie.

"Is there anything I can help you with?" Kit asked. She seemed happy to be not holding a baby.

"No, it's ready if you guys are." Hazel took a step back. Ruston wondered if it made Kit feel slightly unwelcome.

After getting everyone situated, and the kids' plates filled, conversation flowed around general topics of local sports, Thomas and Kit's school, the kids, and the church. Mostly, the women did not participate. The women each attended to their respective children and ignored the other. Like the grown adults they were.

Though the tension was thick between the ladies, Ruston decided the men would clean the table, and the women should go watch the children play, maybe break the ice surrounding them.

Trying not to listen for the women in the other room, Ruston asked, "It seems to be going well between you two."

"It is, so far." Thomas's eyes darted to the living room. He, too, was worried about them being alone.

"How is the kid thing going?" Ruston asked. It was a big issue for his friend. Now it seemed that his decades-long hang-up wasn't as much of a deal for the right woman.

"Okay. They're good kids. It seems the second husband isn't too into being a dad. And since the first one is dead, it's all on Kit. But she can handle it." Thomas put plates in the dishwasher.

"Are you planning on helping her out?" Ruston grinned at his friend's word choice.

"If she will let me," Thomas admitted.

"Are you going to ask if she will let you?"

"Not there yet."

"I think you are, Thomas. I really think you are." He clasped him on the back and hugged his friend, so happy he had finally found the one.

Walking out into the living room, they found Kit holding her youngest in her arms as she made her excuses and started packing up. Ruston had no idea what had happened, and Hazel looked just as confused as everyone else.

The group headed out, and Thomas helped Kit with getting her boys in the car. After a few minutes, Thomas stomped back into the house, not as happy as he had been before he left the house. In fact, he was pissed.

"Did you get to say goodbye to your girlfriend?" Ruston teased him.

"Shut up, Ruston," Thomas said.

"Come on, Thomas, can't you take a joke?" Ruston tried to lighten the mood.

"A joke, Rusty? She ended it, okay? She said she can no longer see me." He grabbed his jacket he hadn't time to put on after Kit had left, and he had followed.

"Wait, Thomas." Ruston followed him out the door.

"No, I just want to get out of here." He was still putting his coat on as he walked into the chilly night.

"What did she say? Can you fix it?" Ruston couldn't believe she would just end it, not the woman who had come here for supper, all smiles for Thomas.

"Kit didn't really think so. She said she can't be friends with your wife," he hissed at Ruston, surprising him with the answer. What had happened between the women?

"Why?" Hazel asked from the doorway, echoing what he was about to ask.

"Because of the accident, I assume. It wasn't just you who was affected by it, Hazel. I wish you would stop acting like it was all about you," Thomas stated.

"I know that. I swear I didn't say anything." She took a step back as if she needed space between her and his words.

"Thomas, leave her alone." Ruston got between his wife and his friend, knowing which side he was on.

"Don't worry, I will." Thomas slammed out of the house, scaring John Henry and making him cry.

Gathering the boy in his arms, he glanced at his wife, whose face had lost all its color. He watched her turn and leave the room without a word. Having no idea what was going through her mind, he had to get the boy settled and then worry about her.

It took longer than he had expected to get the boy sleeping after a night with a new friend. He talked about nothing but Josiah and James. It seemed the women's kids had no problems getting close.

Sliding into bed with his already sleeping wife, he wondered if she was really sleeping. It didn't seem like it. Tonight, for the first time since the wedding night, she wore a nightgown as a barrier between them. It might as well have been a brick wall.

CHAPTER 29

Hazel had sworn to herself that if Kit was in church, she would talk to her. And there she was, beside her mom and Tess. It would be natural to walk up and talk to them. Hazel knew Tess and Dolly Nordskov well, but she was chickening out. Because she was tired of being the reminder of that day.

In the two days since Kit had dumped Thomas, Ruston had been distant. Way more distant than ever. Hazel knew what it meant. He was tired of her. In a little over a month, it was over. She had come between him and his best friend. He didn't like to choose.

John Henry was with Ruston talking to Natalie's dad. The boy was whiny today and wanted to run, but not in church. From across the room, she could see his annoyance at the little boy. Ruston wanted to talk, but John Henry was making it nearly impossible for him to do so. If he would just let him go, the boy would run. Probably to her. But maybe to his new friend Josiah, who was also struggling to get away from his mother and grandmother.

Completely chickening out on talking to Kit, she went across the room and grabbed John Henry from Ruston so he could talk in peace. Or maybe so he wouldn't be reminded how bad it was being married to her and everything that came with her.

Trying to not see the continued annoyance in his eyes as she grabbed the boy from his arms, she carried him away. In the month since Ruston had come into their lives, she had loosened her grip on the boy, letting him be a boy. But maybe Ruston had liked him because he was so controlled. John Henry never acted out in public until now.

At least now she had a few hundred dollars to get started in a new life. Not that it would last more than a week or so, but she had more than she had a month before. Somehow, she was back at square one with no plan to get to square two, if she even knew what square two looked like. Either way, she had no motivation to get there. Looking back, she should have pushed to get a job and be useful to her husband. Instead, she had stayed at home and raised her own son. He wasn't even their son, just hers.

Slipping out the door, she carried John Henry across the road to Ruston's house. The snow from a few weeks before was gone. There would be more soon, but the grass was already dry and brittle beneath her feet. Inside the warm house, she put her son down, who ran to his room to play. He was probably tired of her as well.

Oddly, he had adjusted to having his own room—he didn't seem to miss his mother being beside him as much as she had missed him. Though Ruston being close had made it easier on her, sometimes she missed his little body being close.

Sitting down heavily on the couch, she knew she should be packing and preparing for a life without the man she loved, but she couldn't bring herself to do it. She was a coward. First she was unable to speak to Kit, and now she wasn't leaving when he wanted her gone. Did she really have to hear him say the words? Would that force her to do it? Or would she stall then as well?

With John Henry busy and Ruston still at church, she curled into a ball at the end of the couch and tried to plan a life she didn't want. This was where she wanted to be, married to Ruston and in the town she loved. But she didn't belong there. She was a reminder to many of the past, a past best forgotten. If she was gone, Natalie could move on and Kit could move on. Life could move on.

As she lay there, the door opened. Expecting to see Ruston, she was surprised when Kit walked through the door. Josiah rushed in after her and ran directly to John Henry's room. Sitting up quickly, she wondered what the other woman was doing here.

"Ruston said you were probably at home. Josiah wanted to say hi, and I couldn't get him to stop." Kit shut the door behind her.

"I think John Henry was feeling the same," Hazel agreed, wiping the tears from her face, wishing she wasn't so obvious about crying.

"Are you feeling okay?" Kit lingered by the open door.

"Fine. I'm fine," she lied. Her life was over. How could she be fine?

"Can we talk?" Kit asked and took a step inside, finally shutting the door behind her.

Now was her chance. She had chickened out earlier but had been given a second chance. This time, she wouldn't blow it. She would make everything right before she left. "Kit, I want you to give Thomas another chance. Everyone can see how much he likes you and how good he is with your kids. I think you two could be really happy together," Hazel blurted out. Too late, she realized that maybe that wasn't what Kit had come to talk about.

"Thomas and I have a lot of obstacles in our way." Kit took another few steps toward the couch.

"I'm not going to be one of them. I know I'm a reminder of the past, but I'm leaving. I swear, Thomas and Ruston can be friends again. I won't get in the way of that." Tears again. Damn tears.

Kit looked at her in confusion. "What are you talking about? Where would you go?"

"Away. Ruston is tired of John Henry and me. He realized it the other night that I'm not worth it. He and Thomas have been friends forever, and he doesn't want to lose that. Not for me." She ran her sleeve over her eyes, willing them to stop.

"You mean the same Ruston who told me I was Thomas's Hazel?" Kit unzipped her jacket with a smile.

"I knew he would get tired of me, but I thought I had more time."

"Did you know that I knew Thomas was going to a wedding the same night as I was in October? He said his best friend was marrying the love of his life and that he had been in love with her since the summer. I thought, no way were we going to the same wedding. After all, you had only been engaged for a few weeks. Whirlwind courtship and all." Kit sat down on the coffee table across from her.

"He only married me to save his job. It was either that or leave Landstad. A permanent mark on his record." Hazel admitted the truth, that he didn't love her like others thought he did. It was all a lie.

"Thomas told me he lied to you to get you to marry him. The guy I watched marry you wanted to marry you. That guy was so in love with you he couldn't think straight that day." Kit looked at her and smiled. "For a man who had officiated hundreds of weddings, he messed up the vows three times."

"Why would he lie to me?" She wiped her eyes again, confused.

"Because you're stubborn and would have left town if he hadn't. He didn't want to live without you, and I'm starting to understand what he feels."

"But I'm not worth anything. I have no job and no skills." She had no job because she didn't know how to do anything. She had put her entire self into a job she hated and wasn't very good at.

"You were always the most talented of you three. Hanna told me once she thought you would be a music star one day, and she was going to be your manager." Kit's words surprised her. Her sister had never once said that to her.

"When did she say that?" She needed to know.

"The summer before," was all Kit had to say.

"They were always so much smarter than me."

"You saw them that way. Henry may have been smart, but Hanna was struggling with school. They were not as perfect as you remember them being. With their passing, we were all able to paint them in a better light." Kit's words were true; her siblings had never been perfect until they were gone.

"You didn't know them," Hazel said. She hadn't known Kit beyond that she was a Nordskov before the wedding. She had been around, but they were not close.

"I knew Hanna. Maybe not as well as you did, but I knew her.

Enough that I see her when I see you. To wonder what she would have been like now, if they would still be together? What their kids would have looked like? Yes, it all runs through my head when I see you. But that's not your fault," she added quickly and took her hands. "You have never been at fault for not being in that car. For looking like Hanna. For living."

"It would have been better if it had been me. I have not done anything with my life."

"Tell that to that little boy down the hallway, Hazel. Tell that to Ruston, who doesn't want to live without you. Or the book club, who loves you." She ticked off the people on her fingers.

"But they were going to college. They were going to make something of themselves."

"And maybe they would have fallen flat on their faces—we will never know. All we know is that they had what they had and were happy. I have felt guilty about those months before the accident. I knew that they were drinking and partying, and I even knew that Jamie and Hanna were having sex. But I'm letting go of that guilt because they only had that time. We have the future to look towards, but they only had that day," Kit said slowly and softly, letting the words linger.

"They should have had more time," Hazel whispered and felt Kit hug her. A tight hug.

"But they didn't. We have to be happy with the time they had. Enjoy the memories and forget the guilt." Kit held her close.

"Did she love him? They were having sex, but did she love him?" she asked as Kit finally let her go.

"Yes, I think so." Kit paused and took a deep breath before adding. "She was pregnant, and they were going to keep the baby."

"She never said," Hazel said in shock. Her sister had been pregnant that day? But she was going to college and was going to be a teacher? What about her plans? What about her future? Would she have loved being a mom as much as Hazel did?

"I think they were going to tell everyone the next week. That was what they had told me. But I don't know for sure. They came to me for advice because I had been there. I should have told you before, but I didn't know how you would take it. I didn't want to upset you."

"I wish she would have said. Talked to me."

"I think she would have, one day. But time ran out."

"Four died that day," Hazel whispered more to herself than to Kit, except Kit was so close she heard.

"What?"

"We came into the world as three, and they died as three. I always felt Jamie took my place, stole my place." Now she was thinking that they died together because they were supposed to be together, that she was no longer a part of that group, another group of three without her. Had they all just grown apart by then?

"Hazel, did you ever think that if you had been in that car, you might have lived? Like Natalie? Survived it? Not everyone in the car died."

"No, I would have died with them."

"That's what Natalie thinks, but she lived. I think you would have lived also. After all, he chose you for Ruston."

"You too?" She wished everyone wasn't on this God's plan thing. "Do you think we can get over this?"

"I hope so, Hazel, because I think we accidentally fell for guys who are best friends." Kit hugged her tight, and she swore she was going to make it work. For Ruston. He taken so many chances by choosing her, it was time for her to take a few of her own.

CHAPTER 30

RUSTON HAD STAYED at the church until he saw Kit leave with her young son. When she had walked across the road, he went to see what state his wife was in. He hoped he was right by giving them space and time to clear up what was between them. That they could clear it up.

Hazel had been distant since Friday night, and he had let her have her space. It was the first time in their marriage that he had sensed she really needed space, so he let her have it. But now they needed to talk about it.

Opening the door, he saw Hazel quickly cleaning the toys the two boys must have taken out of John Henry's room. Her eyes met his, and he saw panic cross her face before she grabbed a few more and hurried to the boy's room.

"Ruston!" John Henry ran to him. Smiling at the boy's enthusiasm, he grabbed him into his arms. The boy was jabbering about something Ruston couldn't understand as Hazel came back into the room.

Her eyes darted from the remaining toys to the boy talking in his arms, then back again. In a near panic, she rushed to Ruston and took the boy from his arms. The boy, it seemed, did not want his mom and squirmed immediately to get away from her. Due to his size versus hers, he was able to get free easily—her days of controlling him with strength alone were soon over.

Quickly, she squatted down and grabbed him around the waist and held his body to hers, whispering, "No, leave him alone. He doesn't want us here today. Don't bother him today."

"Let him go, Hazel. He's not bothering me," he stated firmly, unable to control his tone in that moment. He watched her arms instantly let go at his command.

"He's in a mood." Her voice was still at a whisper, using words he had never heard her use. She was still squatting on the floor as the boy ran off, away from them both. But once he was gone, Hazel took off after him, grabbing him up and hurrying into their bedroom. Shutting the door behind her.

Watching her go, he saw the action for what it was. Defensive. This was how she kept the little boy away from her grandparents for years. The moment he started acting like a little boy, she would take him to her room. That tiny room packed with everything she and he owned.

Not anymore.

Never again.

Stomping to the door, he opened it and saw her holding John Henry tight, her eyes wide at him coming into the room. It must have not been something her grandparents would do. "Hazel, he's four. He's acting perfectly normal. Let him go so he can play," he said, and she did, John Henry darting from the room without looking back at them.

"You're tired of him, of me. I can be out in an hour. I have very little here that's mine." She crushed a bear she had picked up to her chest.

"What are you talking about? What makes you think I'm tired of you? That I could possibly be tired of you?" He didn't move for fear she would leave the room as fast as her son had.

Was it Kit? Had she said something? What could she have said?

"When you married me, you didn't realize that you would have to choose between Thomas and me. But you don't. Thomas is your best friend, so I will leave. You don't have to make that decision." Her words came in a rush.

"You are my wife," he reminded her. She was the most important person to him, besides her son.

"A wife you didn't want. You had to marry me, remember? Now that we're married, we can separate quietly, and your job will be safe." She let go of the bear and dropped it on the bed.

What was going on? Why was she suddenly talking like this now?

"I wasn't exactly honest about that. I was told to marry you or stop seeing you. I couldn't stop seeing you, Hazel. This, what we have right now, is what I wanted. Since that party last summer, I have wanted you in my life." He finally went to her, glad she stayed on the bed.

"Kit was right? You lied to me? Why?" Her shoulders slumped in defeat, and he wished he hadn't let the other woman come over. He should have rushed over to get her to leave when he saw her go into the house.

"I don't know what Kit said to you. I lied because I was scared that if I didn't act fast, you would have left town. I couldn't take the chance of losing you. In fact, if you left Landstad, left me, I would have followed you. Wherever you go, I will follow. I am so in love with you, I can't think when you're not near."

She didn't look up from the stuffed animal on her lap.

"That was then. Now I know you're tired of me, of us. I can see it. We're a bother. You've realized we aren't worth the trouble. I am trouble." She toyed with the bear's ears as she spoke, her words focused on it and not looking up at him.

Crouching down, so he was level with the bear, he took her hand. Just one in both of his. Not wanting her to feel trapped, not wanting her to panic.

"I am not your grandparents, Hazel. I will never be them. I love you both, and I am not going to get tired of you. And John Henry is four; I know he's just being a kid. It's something I love about you two being around, something I didn't even know I was missing before I met you."

"But I have all this stuff from my past, and a loud, messy son, and I don't have a job."

"And none of that matters because it makes you, you. I love you. I don't love a simple and uncomplicated Hazel; I love Hazel May, and I love her kid, and I never want to be without them." He hoped she was listening to him, believing him.

"Nobody has loved me. Not for a long time. Even before they died, I wasn't anyone's favorite. Sometimes I felt everyone liked Natalie better than me. When they died, and she lived, I secretly was happy that she didn't get to die with them. Because that was my place. It proved she couldn't take my place. But still, every time I saw Natalie, I would wonder why I wasn't good enough to have been there with them that night, to die with them. Why not me? Why was God punishing me by letting me live?" Her tears ran down her cheeks and into the bear's fur.

Ruston's heart hurt at her anger, her pain at simply not being included in what she felt was her place, beside them in life and death. To not feel blessed that she lived. That she had spent seven years feeling cursed that she lived. That she was being punished.

"You were never meant to be there. You need to be thankful you were lucky to live. To grow up, to have a son, to have friends and family who love you. You were never supposed to die out there with them." He pulled the bear away and pulled her into his arms, needing her to feel the love that she had been missing for years.

Her body burrowed into his, and her tears dampened his shirt. "My grandparents hated that I was a constant reminder that they were gone. They couldn't get over that. I was a disappointment to them, a disappointment that I didn't die. That I brought a baby home. That I continued to live."

Ruston shook his head, though she couldn't see it. "That's their issue, Hazel, not yours. I think that your grandparents were the most negative people I have ever met. In the end, they were just looking for an excuse to not love you because you are easy to love."

"They loved me once upon a time. Growing up, I knew I was loved. We were all loved. It made it harder when the love was gone, replaced by bitterness that nothing could fix. All the pictures were put away, all the memories forgotten. We were all just surviving for so long."

Pulling away slightly, he cupped her cheeks, so she had to look into his eyes, so he could see her as he spoke. Her hazel eyes shimmered with tears ready to fall again. "I don't want you ever to just be surviving, Hazel. I want you to be alive and living. And know that you are loved every day by John Henry, by me, by your friends. You are important to every one of us."

He watched her absorb the words, and her slight smile at John Henry's name made him smile back at her. His thumb ran over her cheeks, wiping the tears away, tears that had finally stopped running from her eyes.

"Did you mess up our vows?" she whispered the question.

"What? I don't know. I don't remember the vows. I was so captivated by the bride I couldn't remember my name." It was the truth—what was said was lost in the beauty of her.

"Kit said you messed them up, but I can't remember." Her words were a little louder, a little bolder.

"I remember everything important about the day, from you climbing into bed with me that morning to climbing into bed with you that night. Everything in between." He kissed a still damp cheek. Because he couldn't not.

Hazel smiled and sniffed, silent for a moment before saying, "I told them about you. The morning before the wedding, I went to the cemetery and told them. That's why I went to your place, to be safe again. You always make me feel safe."

He kissed her other cheek and whispered, "What did you say about me?"

"That I loved you even if they probably wouldn't have. That I didn't care what they thought anyway. That I missed them. That they missed a lot by dying."

"Have you been back?" It had been weeks, and now it was across the road. So close, but still an emotional journey.

"No, but they're not there. It was just cold and dark and lonely there. They are here, in pictures, in memories. I have to remember that they once lived, that they just didn't die. I want to be reminded that they lived for seventeen years, and every day was a day they had. I don't want to ever forget that again. I want to feel happiness when I think of them, not sadness."

"Hazel, let's live that way, like every day is a gift just for us. To make new memories and enjoy those around us. Together."

"I would love that." Her lips brushed his cheek before brushing his lips in a light kiss.

Resting his forehead on hers, he whispered, nearly touching her lips with his, "Can we also live every day without doubt as to how much I love you?"

"Yes, because I love you too. I'm just so afraid you will leave me. Everyone leaves me." Her words nearly broke him.

"I will never leave you, Haze. I want you by my side every day. That if you want to leave Landstad, I will leave with you." He pulled away. He wanted her to know he was serious; if she couldn't stay here, he would leave with her. He would give everything up and start again for her.

"I don't want to leave, Ruston, you or Landstad. This is where we belong," she promised.

"What if the memories become too much here?" he asked. She might do better not being reminded of the past at every turn. They could start over in a new place, with new people and new memories.

"They are here, and I won't leave them. And besides, this is my home; it always has been. It's where I want to raise our son, our kids. I don't even know where we would go if we left." She smiled and blushed that she had called her son theirs and was looking at a future with more kids. Their kids.

"Then we will stay." He finally kissed her, showing her how much he loved her and how much he wanted her. Pulling away, his breathing was unsteady and all he wanted to do was keep going. But he knew John Henry was somewhere in the house.

"Do you have book club tonight?" he asked.

"No." She shook her head.

"Good, then all your friends are free to babysit, because I need you alone and naked tonight." He pulled away and saw her bite her lip.

"Lock the door." She pulled out her phone.

With a shake of the head, he did her bidding, and as the lock clicked, he heard the opening strains to 'Life in a Northern Town.' Then he heard her turn it up as loud as the phone would go.

Turning back to her, he saw she was already pulling off the shirt she had been wearing, looking up she caught his eye. "Make it quick, preacher man, and keep quiet."

With a laugh, he pulled off his own shirt as he rushed to her, loving her giggle as he tossed her onto the bed. He never got tired of that giggle, that smile, and that damn dimple.

The End

Thank you so much for reading Insuppressible . Did you love it? Are you dying to see how Kit and Thomas ended up together? If you didn't notice the two stories overlapped each other. Check out their story in 'Intriguing'.

EPILOGUE

ONE LAST LOOK at the clock, and Hazel knew she was late. Today seemed like one of those days where the past was pressing down on her. Today was her birthday, and not just hers. But today would be the first one she wouldn't spend with her grandma. Over the last few months, she had hoped her grandma would have a change of heart, but so far, that hadn't happened, and Hazel was slowly losing faith that it ever would.

Two weeks ago, she heard that Rose had moved from Landstad to Campbell. It was only seven miles away, but for Hazel, it felt like the rift between them had turned into an ocean. She was sure everyone in town knew before she did, and only Ruston had been brave enough to tell her. But then Ruston was probably the only person she would let herself fall apart in front of.

His parents had tried to take over the role her grandparents once held in her life, but she wasn't ready for them to be replaced just yet. Though she was more than willing to let them be the kind of grandparents her son had never had.

For a moment, she debated on a jacket. It was only a short walk across the street, but it was also fifteen below zero. If she didn't take a jacket, she would freeze, but it was such a hassle for such a short walk.

"Put on a jacket, Hazel." Her grandma's voice rang through her head, and instantly she pulled it from the closet and slipped into it.

The memory was enough to make tears sting her eyes. She knew it would be easier if her grandma was just dead instead of seven miles away. That she had closure and no hope to see her again. Closure was all she needed that day.

Out the door, the cold took her breath away instantly. No matter how many winters she had lived through, the cold surprised her every year. But this year, she was able to go out without explaining where she was going and what she was doing. Whether her grandparents had been nosy or worried, she would never know. They never said. Probably just concerned that she would leave John Henry and never come back.

Putting her head down, she rushed to the church, but instead of the church, her chilled feet took her someplace else, someplace she hadn't been in months and hadn't even thought of as a place where she wanted to go.

Red tennis shoes sank into the half-foot of crunchy snow as she went. Some trickled into her socks, but she didn't feel the cold at all as she stopped and looked at the familiar names—names that she had learned to spell and write as she learned her own. How jealous she had been that neither of her siblings had to learn both e and a in their names, but she did. Had they been just as jealous that she had an L, the easiest letter to write in the alphabet? She would never know.

In the daylight, she felt weird talking to them out loud. In the dark before her wedding, it was easy, but today it wasn't. But now they were not the strangers they had been before. She had made sure that their memory was a part of her present. That they were not forgotten again.

Natalie had helped with that. She had let her back into her life more and more. Or maybe it was that Natalie pushed to be back in her life more and more. Natalie had changed from the girl who had been friends with Hanna. Hazel didn't know whether it was the accident that changed her or if she would have changed anyway. Maybe she would always have matured into the woman she was now. Would

Hanna have matured the same way? Would she and her sister be close? Had Hanna died at a moment when she wasn't a nice person?

"Happy birthday, Hazel," Kit said from behind her, causing Hazel to jump.

Turning, she tried to smile a little and push away the tears that had frozen on her cheeks in the extreme cold. "Thanks. Did Ruston tell you?"

Kit's eyes went to the grave behind her. "No, I saw you. I …"

"You were worried?" Hazel asked in surprise.

"Sort of. It is well below zero, and your jacket isn't even zipped up. That and you never come out here." Kit shoved her hands in her pockets because the woman looked freezing cold already, even if she was in a big fluffy jacket.

"I should. It's right here." She looked over at her house, where she felt more at home in than the one she had been raised in.

"How about when it is warmer? I'll come with. Natalie too. Take a day to remember them," Kit suggested.

"You don't have to say that." Hazel shook her head.

"I know, but I want to." Kit looked back at Thomas. "I told you once, and I will tell you again. You were not the only one affected by the accident. I hurt too."

"I didn't mean it like that," Hazel said. "I just know you are busy with your work, kids, and everything."

"Not too busy for my friends," Kit said. "And I consider you my friend, and not just because Thomas and Ruston are friends. But because we are friends. We are part of a club that has few members, and we must be there for each other."

"What club?" she asked, because Kit was not a part of book club, had never even shown an interest in it. And if she did want in, her sister, cousin, and brother's girlfriend were in it. There was no need to ask Hazel for permission.

"The survivors club. And it's just you, me, and Natalie. For years, we have been trying to get through this alone, but from here on out, we do it together."

"That sounds nice." She watched Natalie tromping through the snow, coming their way.

"Hey, Kit. happy birthday." Natalie instantly enveloped her into a hug. She didn't know if Natalie was talking to her or her sibling's grave. And for once, Hazel didn't care. "I should have come earlier, but Sam takes forever to get ready. Men, right?" Natalie rambled and gave Hazel a hug. "What are you two doing?"

"Forming a club. You're already a member," Kit informed her.

"Can I be president?" Natalie didn't even question the club.

"There are only three of us in it. No president," Hazel informed her, smiling.

"I'm spread pretty thin with softball, the wedding, and the book club, so another club might take a lot of my time." Natalie ticked her responsibilities off on her hand.

"Being the president would take more time than just being in the club," Kit stated in confusion.

"Just tell her she's already in and can't leave," Hazel said.

It was exactly how Natalie treated her.

"How about I tell you all about the club, so Hazel can have a moment alone." Kit grabbed a hold of Natalie's jacket and pulled her toward the church.

Natalie grumbled but went along. Probably because it was freezing out, and Sam was waiting outside the church for her. It was cute how much he adored her, even if she was annoying as hell.

Thomas peeked out the door as they were walking back, and his face lit up when he saw his girlfriend. Hazel was sure there would soon be a Nordskov wedding in the future, and not just for Math and Tess. Thomas and Kit's whirlwind courtship was still making its rounds in town, but not many knew much about it. Not even Mia knew the details, which was rare in a town this size, and Kit was her cousin.

When both couples had gone into the church, Hazel let the cold win and headed for the church as well, but instead of going in the door everyone else did, she slipped around back and walked up the snow-covered steps. Before she could grab the doorknob, it swung open.

Ruston stood in the doorway, his hair combed smooth, and his black slacks pressed, looking exactly like he always did when preaching. It was just as yummy as the first time she saw him here. Stepping aside, he let her into the room and shut the door.

The heat of the room encircled her, and she realized just how cold she was from being outside for so long. Flexing her fingers, she tried to get the circulation back in them.

Ruston just watched her. He had to have been watching her from the window to know she was coming up the stairs. Had he watched the entire time? Had he known she was going to stop and see them today.

"How are you?" he asked quietly as he helped her take off her jacket.

"Good, or maybe okay. Today is always hard," she admitted.

"You can have a bad day, it's okay."

"It's Tess's baby's baptism, I can be okay for that," she assured him.

"I talked Sam and Natalie into taking John Henry for the rest of the day . You can be alone, or we can be alone, or I can cancel." He looked nervous about making a parenting decision without her. Even if it was for her benefit, he had done it.

"That is exactly what I need." She smiled, a real one, probably for the first time today. "Thank you for thinking of me today."

"Hazel, I think about you every moment of every day. From the moment I first saw you, I have thought about you. Even when I barely knew you, I thought about you. Now I think about you from the moment I open my eyes in the morning until I close them at night. You are my world." He pulled her into his arms and held her tight. Exactly what she needed right then.

"You didn't say it was God's plan," she whispered since they were in the church.

"Thank you for saying it." He kissed her hair and continued to hold her.

"I am not turning into a great pastor's wife," she admitted, glad she wasn't looking at him.

He chuckled, and she felt his body shake a little. "You're still changing, Hazel. We all are. And I will love you through every one of them."

"I love you too, Ruston. Even when I didn't want to." She burrowed into his warmth as her phone buzzed in her pocket.

Pulling it out, she didn't want to move but did just enough to ready the text.

Mia: Natalie's room, now.

This time it was her who chuckled and pulled away from him. "I have to go."

"Book club meeting?" he asked, tucking a lock of hair behind her ear.

"Just a toast. Good thing Natalie has everything ready. I'm late." She kissed him quickly and went out the same way she had come in. Because if she went out the other door, everybody already waiting for services to start would see her leaving a room Ruston was supposed to be in alone. There would be gossip even if they were married.

She had been fully accepted as Ruston's wife, and everyone was nothing but friendly. It had taken a month or two to really get used to being married and having someone else to lean on, but Ruston made everything in her life easier.

As she went down the steps, she let herself be happy because she *was* happy. Completely happy with her life.

BONUS EPILOGUE

Eight years. It had been eight years since the day that changed her everything. Today Hazel was spending the day with Natalie for the first time. The entire day. Ruston was to drop her off when he took John Henry to school for the day, leaving her trapped with her old friend. If not for the four-block walk that would take her home, she was stuck here. So maybe not completely trapped.

Standing at the door of Natalie and Sam's little ranch, she wondered if this was a good idea. Today was made for tears, but was she even wanting to share them with Natalie? But Natalie had the same tears. Together they would get through it as best they could.

Today they were celebrating the time Henry, Hanna, and Jamie had, not to mourn the years that they didn't. It had been a trying year of working toward being happy that she had them for as long as she had and not dwelling on what they missed. She realized that she had missed stuff when they were there, not just after they were gone.

Even though Natalie had admitted that she had broken up with Henry, Hazel had not told her Hanna's secret. After all these years, she didn't want Natalie to think that Hanna had kept things from her, that she had secrets she hadn't told her. Hazel was not getting in the way of their friendship, even now, years later.

The door swung open before Hazel even knocked, and Natalie stood there in an oversized Landstad Tiger's T-shirt and matching orange lounge pants. Her usually happy face was frowning at her. "I said wear something comfortable."

Looking down at her own leggings and an oversized sweatshirt, also with a Tiger on it, she said, "This is comfortable."

"But you wear this every day," Natalie complained, but if Hazel was any more comfortable, she would be naked, and that wasn't happening at Natalie's house. They might be friends now, but no matter how many times Natalie suggested switching partners, she wasn't ever going to even think about it. Natalie wasn't either, but it made everyone uncomfortable, so she kept saying it.

"It's not my fault I live more comfortably than you do. Can I come in?" she questioned her friend, wondering if Ruston would come back for her if Natalie really didn't let her in or if she would have to just walk home.

"Yes, I have lounge pants for you if you want them." Natalie waved her in, even as Hazel walked through the door. As friends now, she didn't need an actual invite into the house anymore. Most of the time, Hazel just walked in, but today was different.

"They would not fit me." Hazel eyed her tall friend.

Natalie's eyes narrowed at her, and she folded her arms. "I am going to take that as that you saying you're fatter than me, not because I'm tall. You know how I feel about tall jokes, shorty."

"You are tall, and I am barely fatter than you." Hazel ran her hand over her stomach, which was actually way bigger than Natalie's own. Mostly because Natalie was almost a foot taller than her, and Hazel was two months further along.

Though Natalie had been the first to announce her pregnancy, Hazel had beaten her to it. Ruston had been so excited about the fact that she was carrying his baby they forgot to tell anyone else for over a month. For a God-fearing man, he was sure superstitious about pregnancy.

"Okay, Hazel May, you're skin and bones over there." Natalie rolled her eyes.

Hazel kicked a toy truck as she walked. It was one of many scattered around the room. "Do you ever clean?"

"Why? They just drag everything out after I put it away." She dismissed the criticism. Her adopted boys were way busier, as her grandma used to say, then John Henry ever was.

"What's the plan?" Hazel asked.

"Talk." Natalie pointed at the couch and watched as Hazel sat down, removing a few stuffed toys before she did.

"We talk all the time." Hazel settled a stuffed moose next to her on the couch.

It was true. They usually talked at least once a week, mostly about their kids and what was happening with them. Sometimes about their shared past and something that reminded one or the other about it. Rarely about the accident.

"Not really. We have husbands around butting in all the time. Now we have none of that. How's it going?" Natalie finally plopped down next to her.

"Fine, and you?" Hazel asked warily. Natalie was and had always been an oversharer.

"Great, never better. Well, I go on bed rest after Thanksgiving, but Mandy says I can't take any chances." She tapped her nearly flat stomach. Tall people had it made.

"Did she say why?"

"I'm high risk, so it's just a precaution. Maybe with the next one we can be a little more relaxed." Natalie smiled and tapped her stomach again.

"Next one?" She raised an eyebrow in question.

"With Sam, oh yeah." Natalie giggled.

"Gross, Natalie. He's our teacher." Hazel would never let Natalie forget it, either.

"No, he's my teacher, Hazy. All mine."

"Double gross," Hazel said, not ever telling her friend she didn't see the attraction. He was the same Mr. Sullivan he had always been. Just a teacher.

"Hey, I have to sit every Sunday and have my minister making eyes at you. And it is so obvious now that you play the piano. He has to crane his neck to see you." Natalie crossed her eyes as she said it.

"I know, I don't get to enjoy watching him either," she admitted the truth.

It had only been a few months since the usual piano player had broken her hip, and Hazel had been roped into playing. Since she had been in the congregation, she went with it. Though she hadn't started a Sunday school class or led any prayers, she had started singing. And now she played the piano.

If she hadn't seen the woman herself, she would have suspected Ruston had made up the injury to get her to play. Instead, she complained about it and had Ruston make it up to her every Sunday morning. And sometimes Sunday night.

The congregation had fully accepted Hazel as Ruston's wife. They were far nicer to her than they were to her when she had been a single mom. Which meant that instead of getting closer to those women, she had found a way to include those who were still on the fringes of acceptance. Those were her people, after all.

"At least you've stopped having dirty thoughts in church," Natalie teased her.

"I never," Hazel said in defense.

"You should. Keep some spice in your marriage."

"There is plenty of spice." None of which she was telling her friend about. After all, she was a preacher's wife.

"Tell me about it." Natalie grinned at her.

"None of your business, Beckett."

"That's what Sam calls me when things get spicy," she cackled.

Hazel made a gagging sound.

"Do you want to start with little and work our way up?" Natalie ran her hand over the massive movie collection on the coffee table.

"Your dad has a problem." Hazel looked at all the videos Patrick Beckett had recorded of his only daughter since the day she was born.

"I know. But they're worth so much to me today. Especially today." Natalie jumped up and headed for the kitchen behind them.

"Shall we start with Natalie's first diaper change, or Natalie falls and scrapes her knee?" Hazel picked up the two videos and showed them to her friend. Her dad videoed far too much of the woman's life.

"Nope, I already have first day of school in the machine." Natalie handed her a glass of lemonade. "Next year we drink alcohol, a lot of it."

Both sat on the couch and watched a small dark-haired girl walk into the familiar doors of Landstad Elementary for the first time. She looked small and scared until you saw the rest of her class, who were all shorter and blonder and probably more scared. Within seconds both were pointing out people who they had not seen in years and ones they see all the time. Even Hazel couldn't tell her and Hanna apart in the video. They were dressed alike as they were for years to come.

By the time Ruston came by with lunch, they had hit the awkward middle school years, and Hazel forbid Ruston from looking at the screen until Natalie dragged him in and forced him to watch Hazel sing the national anthem before a basketball game from the sixth grade, her first solo in public. Natalie played great, Hanna not as well, and Hazel spent the game on the bench. All three had unforgettable hairstyles that made them laugh and cry.

Ruston stayed after that, but mostly he was silent beside her. But held her close when it was needed. Though she hated him seeing her teen years, which were not her best, she was happy he was getting to see her siblings in real life. To know what they had really been like.

In the middle of their ninth-grade year, Sam came home after he had dropped all the boys off at Patrick and Faith's for the evening. No need for them all to see this cry-fest. Sam was able to point out interesting things about some of the students and faculty that made appearances on the screen.

As senior year started, Kit and Thomas came in. Though Hazel had known they had been invited for later in the day, she didn't think they would come. The couples were close, but they didn't talk about the past again after Thanksgiving weekend. All were willing to admit nothing they said would change anything, so they just went forward with life.

With the addition of the new couple, Hazel was pinned between Natalie, who was fidgeting, and Ruston. Getting up, she needed to move. The day of crying and laughing had made her stomach hurt. Moving would stop it.

"This is when Hazel had a crush on Jason Hanson. You remember him, Hazel? God, you loved him." Natalie looked at her from the couch as she passed. "Are you okay?"

"Just fine. I think I used too many muscles laughing at you. I'm just all tensed up." Hazel rubbed her stomach in hopes it would stop churning.

"We can stop." Sam grabbed the remote from his wife and paused the TV on Hanna's face during a night of movies at Natalie's house years before.

"No, I'm fine. Just need to stretch."

Sam unpaused the movie, and her sister's words came as clear as she was saying them to her right now. "Love you, Haze, forever."

The camera moved away from her sister, and Hazel stopped watching. She couldn't remember her sister ever saying those words, but there they were. In eighteen years, she had missed so much.

Her stomach must have felt that she wasn't concentrating on it enough because suddenly, her entire body hurt. Breathing in, she whispered, "Fuck."

Ruston was off the couch in an instant. "Haze, are you okay?"

"No, I don't think I am," she admitted, finally starting to worry.

Grabbing her, he lifted her into his arms. "We're going to the hospital."

"I think it's the baby," she whispered, hoping only Ruston heard, but by Natalie's scream, she knew others had heard it.

"Okay, okay," Ruston mumbled.

"We'll take care of John Henry, you two go." Sam grabbed coats and tossed them at the couple.

"We're not due for another month," Ruston said as he carried her out of the house.

"It's probably nothing. Just the day," Hazel said, but she was afraid the day was too much for her.

But she knew nothing good had ever happened on this day, so having a baby on it would be good. She only hoped she could hold out until tomorrow if it was wanting out.

* * *

Hale Ruston and Hattie May Hanna Abbott were born just before midnight, at nearly the exact moment eight years after the accident that took their aunt and uncle from them. The two-hour drive from Landstad had been made in half the time it should have taken. Thanks to a call of Kit's, they had a police escort the entire way. But labor was too far gone, and the surprise twins had made the saddest day in their mother's life a little better.

Not that twins were a surprise to either of their parents since Mandy had told them from the very beginning it was two. But they had not shared that with anyone, so it was a surprise.

Ruston couldn't be happier with the babies, though he wished they looked a little more like his beautiful blonde wife. These two already had darker hair and eyes than their big brother.

"How are you?" He sat on the bed and ran a hand over her messy hair, so gorgeous after having two babies the night before.

"Good, worried I should have stayed home yesterday. Too much emotion."

"Everything worked out perfectly, Hazel."

"Don't say it."

"God has his plans," he said anyway as she rolled her eyes at him. It had taken time for him to see her view on religion was slightly different than his, but it was working for them.

"I wanted another month," she argued.

"He wanted to replace your twins with twins. Full circle. I think you were going to have them yesterday no matter what you did." He smiled at her second eye roll. But he was sure that this was how it was going to happen all along.

"You're so cheesy," she said with a dimpled smile.

"You're so cute." He still loved to see them, though they came out far more now than they had before. He was happy and surprised every time he saw them.

"I'm sure I am, with my hair sticking everywhere." She touched it with her hands.

He touched it too. "It reminds me of a night not so long ago when I danced with a woman with spiked hair. It turned out pretty good."

"Because you had dirty sex in the middle of a house party?" Instantly, she blushed and looked around the room to make sure nobody was there.

Kissing her lips, he replied, "Because I got you. And now we are a family of five. Two at a time makes the numbers climb quickly. First, I got you and John Henry, and then these two. What's next?"

"I guess only your God knows. It's his plan, after all." Her words warmed his heart because she said them way less sarcastically than she used to, almost like she believed them. He was sure that in time, she would. In her own time.

"And what a plan it is, Hazel May."

The End

Non-Book Club member and sister to Mathias and Amanda Nordskov, Kit Kittson falls for a playboy teacher in <u>Intriguing</u>.

ALSO BY ALIE GARNETT

<u>Indulge</u>

Craving Winter

Enticing Aurora

<u>Landstad, ND</u>

Invisible

Irresistible

Impulsive

Insuppressible

Intriguing

Imperfect

Irreplaceable

<u>The Great Lovely Falls</u>

Falling for the Single Mom

Falling for his Best Friends Sister

Falling for the Boss

Falling for his Step-Sister

Falling for his Fake Wife

Falling into a Second Chance

<u>Hart Series</u>

Seeing her Pain

Her Favor

Max Valentine is Looking at Me!

Keeping her Safe

ABOUT THE AUTHOR

I love to read and prefer a little spice in those books. I am lucky enough to live on a small hobby farm in northern Minnesota with her husband and two kids. I enjoy spending time in the pasture with my two mini horses and one fainting goat (who doesn't actually faint). When I'm not writing, I'm busy trying to do all the things I didn't get to while writing. Or maybe I wouldn't have gotten to them anyway, because its laundry, dishes and fun things like that.